WELCOME TO WEST STREET

BOOKS BY NICOLE TROPE

Standalone Novels

My Daughter's Secret

The Boy in the Photo

The Nowhere Girl

The Life She Left Behind

The Girl Who Never Came Home

Bring Him Home

The Family Across the Street

The Mother's Fault

The Stepchild

His Other Wife

The Foster Family

The Stay-at-Home Mother

The Truth about the Accident

The Day After the Party

His Double Life

Grace Morton Series

Not a Good Enough Mother

A Mother Always Knows

NICOLE TROPE

WELCOME TO WEST STREET

bookouture

Published by Bookouture in 2025

An imprint of Storyfire Ltd.
Carmelite House
50 Victoria Embankment
London EC4Y 0DZ

www.bookouture.com

The authorised representative in the EEA is Hachette Ireland
8 Castlecourt Centre
Dublin 15 D15 XTP3
Ireland
(email: info@hbgi.ie)

ISBN: 978-1-83618-664-9
eBook ISBN: 978-1-83618-663-2

For D.M.I and J

PROLOGUE

She forces one foot in front of the other, sweat coating her skin as she makes her way along the tree-lined street.

Large houses are just visible in the silent darkness. Night-blooming jasmine covers high walls, the scent drifting through the warm air. A dog barks in the distance and for a moment she freezes, thinking this could end everything – but thankfully, all falls quiet.

There was so much blood. How is it possible there was so much blood?

She never thought she would be strong enough. She imagined he would stop her. But he didn't. Instead, *she* stopped *him* with a single blow.

He toppled forward, the blood sinking into the carpet, spreading into a large, plum-coloured puddle.

And then he lay still. Very, very still.

Now she just needs to get out of here, her steps heavy, her mind whirling, shock making her shiver. How could she have done that? What kind of a person can do something like that?

Despite the late hour and the quiet, she is certain someone must be watching. People are always watching in places like this. Somewhere behind a closed curtain, someone is probably calling the police and reporting a woman staggering along their perfect street, dark patches of blood on her clothes.

She turns her body slightly, her muscles aching, trying to see behind her.

She needs to get to her car, needs to get somewhere safe, away from prying eyes.

How has it come to this? How has she come to this?

And what's going to happen now?

ONE
TWO WEEKS AGO

Amanda

She can't help the wave of despair that washes over her as she navigates her black Mercedes into the rutted driveway. The bricks need replacing and she can see from the outside of the small house that it needs to be repainted. The walls must have been white at some point but have discoloured to a dirty cream, and whole sections of paint have peeled off, exposing the brick underneath.

'It's not forever,' she whispers.

'What did you say?' asks Kiera.

'Nothing, sweetheart, nothing. I thought you were watching the *Barbie* movie,' she replies, offering a quick smile to her nine-year-old daughter before turning back to stare at the tired little house.

'I've watched that like a gazillion times, Mum,' says Kiera and even though she's not looking at her, Amanda knows that Kiera is rolling her eyes. It's something she's started doing recently and she does it with drama and flair. Amanda can't help smiling when she sees it although she knows she may one day regret that reaction.

She takes her phone out of her bag and texts her sister, not caring what time it is in the UK. Paula will answer anyway. She always answers.

Please tell me I'm doing the right thing.

You're doing the right thing. Just breathe.

But Paula doesn't know everything that Amanda is doing. Because there are some things Amanda has kept all to herself.

Even so, she follows her sister's instruction and takes a deep breath as she glances in the rear-view mirror. Jordan is still playing his game, his blue eyes concentrated on his screen as his hands move quickly across it, killing something no doubt – an alien, a robot, a troll.

Opening her car door, she steps out into the January warmth, squinting against the bright sun, and then she grabs her bag, fishing out the keys the real estate agent handed her a week ago.

'We're here, Jordan, we're here.' Amanda turns to see Kiera shoving her brother, something she would usually tell her daughter to stop doing but Kiera is doing it gently and with a smile. Her daughter looks like Amanda did as a child, with the same brown hair and brown eyes, but Jordan is his father's mini-me, in more ways than one.

'Stop it,' he barks, 'just stop it, I'm winning.'

She opens her mouth to say something but finds she doesn't have the energy to tell him not to be rude, not today.

Making her way to the front door, she notices the overgrown grass in the front garden, remembering that the estate agent said that someone would be out this week to tidy it and also remembering the way the young woman had looked at her when she enquired about renting the house without seeing it.

'Are you sure? It's like over an hour away from here and it's quite run-down,' she said, pushing her long blonde hair behind her ears. 'The owners just want to rent it for six months before they start building. We can't do many repairs and that's why the rent is so cheap,' she continued as though Amanda just needed to understand what kind of a place she was hoping to rent and then it would be instantly dismissed as a bad idea. The estate agent had looked down at Amanda's shoes, noticing the soft leather of her sandals, and then glanced at her bag, seeing the obvious, over-the-top designer label. Amanda had stood patiently, enduring the scrutiny. She had only just come from the hairdresser so her streaked brown hair had been lying in waves across her shoulders, and her sunglasses with their shiny entwined Cs were perched on top of her head. The other woman couldn't have known how fast her heart was beating, how scared she was of being spotted standing in the office with large glass windows that looked out onto the small side street. And she couldn't have known what it had taken for Amanda to walk in there in the first place, how many months of planning and worrying.

She couldn't have known that inside Amanda's head there was a message on repeat, a text message. A message that she had never expected to receive and one that had made her question her whole life and everything she knew to be true.

You don't know me but...

On the outside, she was coiffed perfection but inside, she was a mess.

'It's fine,' she replied. 'It's what I want. I can pay for six months upfront.' The woman's look of shock was almost comical. And when Amanda took cash out of her bag, thousands of dollars bundled together with elastic bands, it was clear the agent really wasn't quite sure what to do. No one carried cash around anymore except for drug dealers and criminals.

Is what she's doing a crime? No, what she's doing is necessary. It is necessary that she is here, in this small house, far away from the house she called home for the last twelve years.

'Um... I need to get my... I'll be back,' the estate agent said after staring at the cash, and Amanda sat down in a nearby chair to wait, her knees suddenly feeling week. Her jaw was tense, her back muscles felt like they were in spasm. Her whole body wanted to turn and run but she would not leave. She thought about Kiera and Jordan, who were both enjoying a day with friends, their whole summer stretching before them. Christmas was over, presents unwrapped, pictures taken and now a new year had begun. And she was hoping for a new Amanda to go with it.

You don't know me but...

Amanda knows now. She knows everything.

Her children would not be happy about the house and she knew that. But she was doing what she had to do.

Now she pushes the key into the lock, turning it and then giving the front door a shove when it doesn't open easily. The wood is swollen from recent rains so she hopes it will work better when it dries out. According to the weather bureau there are only sunny skies ahead for the next three weeks.

'Sunny skies ahead,' she says aloud as Kiera runs through the house to the back and she walks through slowly, opening curtains and windows. The house is old but it's not in a dreadful state. It actually looks better than she imagined it would look based on the pictures she had seen on the internet. The vague smell of mould is overlaid with the smell of disinfectant but, hopefully, that can be sorted out with long warm days. She has never lived somewhere like this and she thinks briefly of her living room at home where the caramel-coloured leather sofas are adorned with cream pillows to match the plush cream carpet.

That's not home. Not anymore.

'Why are we here?'

Amanda turns to find Jordan standing behind her, his backpack over his shoulder and his iPad in his hand. She looks up, amazed as she is every day that her eleven-year-old son is taller than she is. Taller than and probably stronger, certainly angrier if the scowl on his face is any indication. It seems that this is Jordan's permanent expression these days and Amanda wonders when she last heard him laugh. He doesn't even try to hide his disdain for his mother anymore. 'Wait until he's a teenager,' her friend Valerie told her when she complained about Jordan's behaviour. Amanda knew Jordan was going to get worse, much worse, and that's partly why she's here, in this small house, in a suburb an hour away from her large comfortable home. Former home. Valerie has no idea of the influences in Jordan's life.

'I told you. We're going to stay here for a while.'

'Why? This is a dump. There's no pool. Why are we here?'

'It's because of the fighting,' says Kiera, coming in from the garden she has been exploring. 'Isn't that right, Mum?'

Amanda nods because why lie? 'That's right, baby, because of the fighting.' And so much more than that.

'So you fight with Dad and we have to move?' he spits. 'I hate this. I hate you,' he says and he stomps off to find his room. The words are a gut punch, painful and harsh. They wipe away the thousands of 'I love you, Mummys' she has heard from him. He sounds like an angry man, but he is still just a boy. He doesn't hate her. He hates himself as he grapples with unfamiliar emotions and he hates that his life has suddenly changed. How else can he express it? She should reprimand him, tell him about the power of words, make him understand why he shouldn't say things like that, but he won't listen, not now. He is too confused, too upset for her to try and discipline him now.

This is not my fault. I wish I could explain it to you but it's not my fault.

'Stop being mean to Mum,' shouts Kiera and she is answered with the slam of a bedroom door. Amanda wants to call after him, to tell him to take the bigger bedroom because Kiera will be fine with the smaller one. Kiera is her sunshine child, mostly happy, always kind and ready to help. She wants to protect Amanda, even at her young age, she wants to make things better for her mother. Her daughter wants to save her and her sister wants to save her but Amanda knows that only she can do this. She has done this.

Outside she hears the sound of the small moving truck pulling up and she takes a deep breath, remembering her sister's advice.

I'm doing the right thing.

The truck is filled with cheap, utilitarian furniture. She has left everything behind but her clothes and jewellery, stuff for the kitchen and the children's things.

She hopes that he will understand her meaning, will understand why she has left behind all her beautiful things. *You can have everything else if you just let me do this. Let me go.*

Will he understand? Will he let her go?

Amanda knows he doesn't really care about things. He cares about control.

She moves towards the front door to greet the movers even as a phrase circles in her head, something she has heard her husband say so many times, it's become part of her psyche.

If you leave me, you'll regret it. I promise you; you'll regret it.

TWO

Caroline

I am sitting with Mary in her front room, enjoying our regular morning cup of tea, when the slamming of a car door alerts us to the presence of someone in the cul-de-sac.

'Another delivery for Gemma?' asks Mary with a smile. Gemma is at work but Mary and I are used to her packages arriving throughout the day. She is fond of online shopping.

I stand and go to the window, twitching aside the faded blue curtains to see.

Here at the bottom of the road, far away from the main highway, the days are quiet and the nights filled with the sounds of insects and bats. The noise from the highway is a continuous whooshing sound, making me think of waves, so it's actually quite peaceful. And it's important that we maintain that peace and that means watching out for each other, watching who comes and goes.

'There's a car in the driveway of Cora's old house,' I tell Mary. 'Large and black, looks expensive.'

'So it's been rented then. I thought it would take longer.'

The house across the road from mine was bought three months ago for more money than I would have believed.

West Street is a newish street, if you consider a street developed in the 1980s new. The suburb of Delmont used to be just bush until the bulldozers arrived and little boxes of homes were built so everyone could have their own Australian dream of owning a property.

'I've never understood those oversized cars. My little sedan gets me where I need to go just as well without guzzling litres of petrol,' I say as I watch a woman climb out of the Mercedes. She has streaked brown hair and is wearing large sunglasses that cover most of her face. She looks... expensive is the best word I can use to describe her, well put together, nicely dressed even in jeans and a blue shirt.

'Well?' asks Mary, frustrated at my silence. She would be standing here next to me if she could, and I can't help but remember her ten years ago when she was still strong and looked like she would be forever. She walked with a small limp then. 'I fell off a bicycle,' she told me when I first asked about it. 'A car accident,' she has also said and, 'I fell out of a tree as a child.' Her knees have bothered her more and more as she has aged, and now she can only get around with her rather cumbersome walker.

'It's a woman. I'm sure she can't have rented the house. She doesn't look the type. Oh, and wait, there's a little girl as well, so sweet, reminds me of Janine when she was that age, around nine or ten I think.'

At nine my Janine was a delight but the teenage years brought so much trouble. She became argumentative over everything, difficult to talk to, and I could do nothing but wait for the stage to pass. I remember when she would change her hair colour every few weeks. Liam and I never knew what she was going to come up with next. I did warn her that all the chemicals weren't good for her but you cannot argue with a teenage girl, and now that she's in her thirties, she's let her hair return to its original honey colour, just like mine used to be before I went grey. I never coloured my hair. I was happy to earn my grey. I am seventy and I look seventy and that's fine with me. People tend to dismiss or ignore an older woman, and although I have heard many women my age bemoan this, it suits me.

'They're all sweet at that age,' says Mary.

'Oh, and wait, a boy as well, tall, goodness me very tall but he looks quite young, definitely not a teenager yet.'

The boy, who has sandy-blond hair, looks around, holding his iPad in one hand. Even from here I can see his scowl. Like his sister, he is dressed in shorts and a T-shirt but she's wearing pink sandals and he is wearing a giant pair of lurid green and yellow sneakers. It's the fashion of the day I suppose.

'He's not happy,' I tell Mary as he stomps into the house after his mother and sister. 'They're definitely moving in. A moving truck has pulled up now. I wonder why on earth they chose to rent here.'

'What's the husband look like?'

Craning my neck, I search for a man who could be the husband but I can't see anyone. 'No husband.'

'Ah, a broken family,' says Mary.

'There are so many of them around,' I agree. 'I mean, he could be at work but moving days are important. One imagines he would be here. But she really is not who I imagined would rent the house at all.'

I leave the window and return to my tea.

'Well, everyone has their own story,' muses Mary. 'Perhaps she's running from something or someone.'

'I have no idea but I think that if she is, she's in the best place. It's a good street to find yourself on if you need some help.'

'It is,' Mary agrees because she knows we look out for each

other on the cul-de-sac, me and Gemma and Mary. We looked out for Cora as well before her son drove her to an early grave by forcing her out of her house – the house the new family have just moved into.

Mary is ten years older than I am but it feels as though we have the same opinions on most things, and even though Gemma is much younger, we all get along so well. In my experience it's much easier to spend time with someone who thinks the same way you do. I wonder if the new neighbour will fit in here, if she will like it and if we will like her.

'Well, we'll be here to help if she needs it,' I say, standing up and taking the tea things to put them in the dishwasher.

'Oh, we will be,' agrees Mary.

'I'll make them a cake to welcome them.'

'Good idea. They'll like that.'

With that, I leave Mary watching television and return home.

It's been my home for over ten years and it suits me just fine, despite the lack of large trees to bring shade like they do in older, more established suburbs. What drew me here was, mainly, the price. I was on my own and even though I had my husband's life insurance, it wasn't very much at all. I have the smallest house on the street but it does have enough space for me and a place where I can store my bottles of pickled vegetables. Pickling is a process that both engages and soothes me and I do love the taste of pickled cucumbers, radishes and peppers. I give them away for Christmas to the others in the street, some of whom appreciate them more than others, I'm sure.

'There's a new family in Cora's house,' I tell Luna, who is curled up on a chair.

My cat blinks and yawns, the goings-on of the street being of no real interest to her, unless perhaps the family have a cat as well. She shakes her midnight-black head at me and then curls up tighter and returns to sleep. This morning, I woke to find a half-dead mouse next to my bed and I had to put the poor thing out of its misery. Luna stalks the neighbourhood all night and frequently brings me back disgusting presents but I can't be upset at her. It's in her nature and you can't fight nature.

I found Luna in my garden one morning five years ago, just a tiny curled-up kitten all alone. I couldn't believe anyone would abandon such a precious creature and even though I wasn't sure that I wanted to have the responsibility of a pet, it didn't feel right to let her go to a shelter. Perhaps if she was older, I would have felt less of a connection to her, but she was so small and defenceless and her wide yellow eyes reminded me of the moon, so I almost instantly started calling her Luna and it's hard to let an animal go once you've named it.

It does mean that I have something to talk to. I would hate to be all alone all the time, simply talking to myself.

I suppose we all end up alone anyway. I never expected Liam to die so early and I also assumed that Janine would always live near me but she's in a different state, pursuing her own life with her husband Mark.

I make my way to the kitchen, where I will bake something to welcome the new family to the street, the same way I was welcomed when I moved here.

Then, it was Mary who came over with a sponge cake and a smile for a new neighbour, and now I'm the one who helps Mary. Her mind is still sharp although she does have her odd moments, and her body seems to be slowing down more and more.

West Street is a nice quiet street, a friendly street, and I hope the woman and her children will feel very at home here. I will make a chocolate cake, I think – children love chocolate.

And taking over a cake allows me to ask some questions. I have reached an age where I have accepted my tendency towards nosiness. I like to know people's stories. I like to know who I'm living next door to and across the road from and there's nothing wrong with that.

I pull out my old recipe book, the pages coming out of the faded blue leather-covered notebook, and I page through, finding Janine's favourite cake. I know the recipe by heart of course but the book came from my mother and I like to feel close to her when I bake.

My mother didn't have an easy life. Marriage to a man like my father affects everything and I remember some cruelty from my mother when I was a child. She would randomly pull my hair or pinch me and then get furious if I cried. Now that I'm older, so much older, and I have been married myself, I realise that those moments were because my father had hurt her in some way, either verbally or physically. Cruelty trickles down in families from the strongest to the weakest.

The one place where she was never unkind was in the kitchen and my best memories of childhood involve cooking and baking with my mother.

I wonder if the new neighbour bakes with her daughter or perhaps even her son. I wonder why she's alone and how long she has been alone. I wonder if she is already dating someone new or if she will choose to stay alone. I wonder if she has family near or far away. I have so many questions for her. I am interested in people and there's nothing wrong with that.

I can't wait to get to know her. And for her to know us, me and Mary and Gemma – or 'the ladies of the cul-de-sac', as Mary dubbed us a few years ago.

'Better than the housewives of the cul-de-sac,' Gemma laughed.

'Nothing wrong with being a housewife,' I told her. 'Housewives keep the world running.'

'Amen to that,' said Mary.

Whoever the new neighbour is, I'm sure we'll all get along and it's always nice to meet someone new. She's sure to like us and want to become part of our little group. It's impossible to keep to yourself down here. We're just not those sorts of neighbours. We are the sort who are involved in each other's lives. I'm sure she'll quickly learn to appreciate that and to appreciate us. And if she doesn't... well, perhaps this is entirely the wrong street for her. And that would be a shame.

THREE

Amanda

It's after two by the time the moving men have left, and Kiera is in her room, unpacking her toys and clothes. Amanda can hear her singing along to something on her iPad.

When she left her house, it seemed that she had brought so very little with her but now that the boxes are everywhere, piled in each room on the clean but stained beige carpet, she can't believe how much there actually is. She keeps starting on a box and then leaving it to move on to another because the task feels too immense.

Just get one thing done.

'Jordan,' she calls, 'can you come and help me set up the television?' She knows that's pretty much the only thing that will get him out of his room. He is supposed to be unpacking but she knows he's gaming. The television is new and very large but it was cheaper than she expected it to be. It will not compare to the home theatre system Jordan is used to, but hopefully he'll be able to play the video games he loves. It's three weeks until school starts and Amanda knows that wherever he is, Jordan will spend the day playing online with international *friends*. He used to go out with his skateboard, he used to like swimming, he used to play basketball but now he just plays video games with people from all over the world and he barely ever sees the boys he's at school with, claiming they are all 'lame'.

'Boundaries need to be put in place to stop children gaming,' an article she read informed her, but she hasn't done that. She is not good with boundaries, obviously, or she wouldn't be here in this suburb and this house. It's her intention to do things differently once school starts, to begin with new rules and to run her small family the way she wants to, but right now, she can't stop the gaming. She doesn't have the energy to police it or the fortitude to deal with what will be just one extended argument that will go for days and days.

She has taken her son away from the home he loves and the life he is used to. He's at such a difficult time in his life as he navigates the beginning of puberty and now this move. The world is filled with rules for him to follow and he's at the mercy of the adults around him. She can imagine his frustration.

He refused to pack his clothes and his things this morning, just sat while she threw everything into boxes, helped by the two moving men, Rafe and Charlie. Both of them seemed unfazed by how little she was taking, by how fast she was working to get everything done.

'Only these two bedrooms and the kitchen,' she told Rafe, who is bald with a long white beard and tattooed muscles.

'Yeah, I get it,' he said, nodding his head. She wondered how many times they had seen this kind of a situation before but she was afraid to ask.

'I'm not going anywhere,' Jordan tried when they were ready to leave but she had grabbed his precious iPad and taken it to the car, forcing him to follow along. There's no one at home to take care of him anyway.

What would he have said if she'd shown him the text message? *You don't know me but...* She would never do it. He's too young to have to deal with what it means but would he understand her reaction? Would he be shocked or horrified? Would it break his heart? All those things she imagines, and that's why the message is only for her to read, and reread, allowing it to make her question everything.

She will let him game as much as he likes and deal with it when school starts. She needs to get through the next few weeks and then she can make plans for the future, something she has little idea of right now. What will life look like in a week, three weeks, a month, a year?

She realises that five minutes have passed since she called her son. That's why she's not getting anything done, she keeps getting lost in her own thoughts.

'Jordan,' she calls again and she hears him swear loudly because she has interrupted a game. Despite his complaints about there being no pool here, she knows that he barely used the beautiful landscaped pool at home when he had the opportunity. His gaming is a source of constant arguing between the two of them, but it's not just gaming, it's everything, and she fears that things are going to get much, much worse. Two weeks ago, when she asked him to take out the garbage for her and then kept pestering him until he did it, he hauled the bag out of the bin and on his way out hissed the word 'bitch' at her. His father's word. His father's tone. And a word that a mother should never hear from a son, especially one who is still so young.

Since then, the word is making an appearance more and more often.

'Jordan,' she calls a third time. He opens his bedroom door and stomps over to her.

'Why can't you do this yourself?' he says when he is standing in front of the box she has opened.

'It's too heavy for me to lift alone and you're the internet genius. It needs to be connected to the Wi-Fi.'

'We wouldn't have to do any of this shit if we were still at home.'

She ignores the swear word. Just for now. 'I know and I'm sorry but we're here now and we need to make the best of it.'

'When's Dad getting back from overseas?' He juts out his chin. He believes that his father's return will simply make all this go away. He believes his father can do anything. *And that's the problem because Mike thinks he can do anything as well.*

'In a week,' she says, not wanting to tell him that this question sends a shudder through her body.

Together they lift the television out of the box and then set it up on the white timber sideboard with cross-hatching on the doors and simple metal handles. The sideboard doesn't have the rich smell of timber that her furniture at home has. Instead, it smells of chemicals and paint. She chose everything so quickly, just ordered it all online and had it sent to the storage unit she had set up, that she didn't remember what half of it looked like. But she does know that none of it was expensive, that none of it was chosen with the same care that she chose her furniture at home with. *This is home now*, she reminds herself but it doesn't seem possible.

'Can you take it from here?' she asks him once the television is positioned on the sideboard. 'I need to get on with the kitchen.'

Jordan doesn't answer, just stares at the television, and she can't help her irritation at his silence. 'Jordan, I asked you a question.'

'Does Dad know where we are?' he asks, turning towards her, looking at her with his father's blue eyes.

She doesn't want to lie, so she doesn't answer him, just walks away to the kitchen. She knows she will need to explain, to say something to the children, but she has done everything in such a rush.

Mike is on his way to China. He will spend the week meeting with suppliers and having lovely dinners and buying jewellery for his store. She thinks about how he won't contact her or will just send a message every few days – *Just telling you I'm fine* – because he likes her to miss him and not know where he is or who he's with.

He has no idea where his family are. He doesn't even know they've left.

And then she thinks about him getting home and going straight from the airport to the store because he always does that. She sees him walking into the back office that she knows so well because she used to be a saleswoman in the store, sales girl actually, because at twenty-one you're still a girl and scarcely ready to be out in the world. And then she thinks about him seeing the large yellow envelope on his desk that contains the divorce papers.

Picking up a knife to slice open a box of crockery to unpack, her mind refuses to go to what will happen then.

She lifts a stack of white plates out of the box and places them on the counter while she checks to see if the shelves in the cupboards are clean. The estate agent said that cleaners would be sent in before they arrived and she's grateful to see they have been thorough. The cupboard shelves with their cream laminate door are clean and smooth.

She puts the plates on a shelf near the stove, which is thankfully new – cheap and a brand she has never heard of, but new. The replacement of that and the dishwasher were the only things she insisted on. She couldn't bear the idea of using such an old stove. Even in the pictures the rust on the door and the top was obvious. When the blonde estate agent brought her older boss to speak to Amanda, his eyes went to the bundle of cash she was holding, and after a quick call to the owners, the deal was done. Money doesn't just talk; it shouts and screams and demands you bend to its will. Six months' rent from the secret sale of four designer bags and five pieces of white-gold and precious stone jewellery and here they are. In the last few months, Amanda has become a thief, stolen what technically belonged to her but only technically because everything she owned was at Mike's discretion. Sometimes she received a gift only to find it had disappeared overnight because she 'didn't seem to really love the bag' or 'the necklace' or 'the bracelet'. Mike liked her to be grateful for the beautiful things he bought her.

She has brought most of the kitchen stuff, knowing that Mike will never cook for himself. Her ability to cook was one of the first things that attracted Mike to her.

Amanda has no desire to reminisce but as her hands work on unpacking the boxes and organising the kitchen, she's unable to stop herself. She keeps going back to the start of her and Mike because she's still trying to work out exactly how she got here.

She went to university to study English literature with the lofty ambition of getting a job in publishing, but when she graduated, jobs in publishing were thin on the ground and her mother encouraged her to go into teaching.

'I have no desire to do that,' Amanda told her.

'Then you will have to get a job while you figure out what you do want to do,' her mother replied. 'In this house you are either at university or you have a job.' Her parents had a modern marriage, both of them working as teachers and both of them contributing to the household. If they were alive now, she would be with them, would have run to them for safety and protection. If they were alive now instead of both being gone, her mother dying a year after her father, she would have left sooner, been bolder and less afraid to... She shakes her head – *Don't go there* – as she begins on a box of glassware. 'There's no use thinking like that,' she says aloud.

Her job search took longer than she thought it would but finally, she got an interview in a large jewellery store.

Amanda stops what she's doing, a glass in her hand, as she remembers walking into the store fourteen years ago, remembers the wood-panelled walls and the rows of glass and timber display cases and the giant chandelier that hung in the centre. Everything about the store screamed money. None of the jewellery had price tags, the implication being that if you needed to ask the question, you couldn't afford the merchandise.

She was interviewed by the store manager, Patricia, a tall woman with a soothing voice who was dressed in an elegant black two-piece suit, and who offered Amanda the job. Patricia is still there today, despite being near seventy. She adores Mike and she loves the job. She sees the Mike that everyone sees, everyone but Amanda. Mike is a master of disguise and she knows that not a single one of her friends would believe her if she explained what he was really like behind closed doors.

She thought she had been hired to work in the jewellery store because she was so impressive but Patricia later wryly confessed to her that it was because she was attractive. 'Men tend to spend more when buying from a pretty girl,' she admitted and Amanda knows that she should have been insulted but she wasn't. It was nice to be considered pretty, especially after she met Mike.

She only met him after she had already been working for two weeks. He'd been away on a buying trip. When he came in, she was standing in front of a display case of bracelets, beautiful combinations of diamonds and emeralds and sapphires, just moving the pieces into different positions because Patricia had instructed her to continually change the displays when the store was quiet.

She had no idea who he was, so when a man approached her counter, she stopped what she was doing, carefully locked the case and looked up with a wide smile on her face. 'Can I help you find a beautiful piece for someone special in your life?' she asked him and he laughed.

'I think I could probably find my own, thanks,' he said, holding out his hand. 'I'm Mike, the owner. Patricia tells me you've been a wonderful addition to the store.'

'That's me,' she mutters now as she picks up the knife to slice open another box, 'a wonderful addition.'

She was flustered, not just because she had made a mistake but because he was so good-looking, with neatly cut blond hair and bright blue eyes. He had broad shoulders in a perfectly tailored suit and wore a thick gold wedding ring on his left hand. He was ten years older than her and she was almost instantly smitten with him.

She begins fitting cutlery partitions into the kitchen drawers as she remembers his wedding ring. She should have instantly put him out of her mind, should have even resigned the next day because she was so attracted to him, but she was twenty-one years old and knew nothing about life, nothing about love. She'd had boyfriends but only casually and usually for a short time. All she knew was that she wanted Mike, instantly and completely.

I took another woman's husband but is the punishment fitting? Have I paid the price? Have I been punished enough?

The text message is on repeat in her head and she shakes it away.

Under her T-shirt, the bruised skin on her side throbs as she moves, a pain she is used to. *Have I been punished enough?*

Mike knew she was attracted to him. He saw it from the moment they met.

She never even felt guilty about sleeping with him because by the time that happened, she had spent many nights doing stocktake and bookwork with him as he detailed how awful his wife Annette was, how much he regretted marrying her because she didn't want children, how cold his house felt because she was always out with friends.

There was a rule in Amanda's house that once she and her sister were over sixteen, they each cooked dinner for the family two nights a week. Paula usually threw something together that would only take a few minutes like pasta with sauce from a jar, but Amanda enjoyed cooking, loved finding new recipes for her family to try and always enjoyed their obvious delight at whatever she made.

The first time she and Mike slept together – or had sex in his back office on the leather sofa – was on a Tuesday night. That morning, she'd brought in leftover lamb shanks with roast potatoes. She had forgotten that her parents and Paula would be out and so had catered for the whole family. Instead of leaving the food at home, she'd decided to share it with her workmates. Obviously, she was trying to impress Mike, who had told her he lived on takeaway because Annette never cooked.

It worked. At lunch, he sat down in front of a plate and ate every last bite and then said, 'You will make some lucky man a wonderful wife, Amanda. I wish I'd met you earlier. I wish I was younger so that man could be me.'

As she picks up a handful of knives, feeling some of the blades press into her palm, Amanda remembers her flippant reply. 'You're not so old and you've met me now,' she said with a laugh.

So arrogant, so sure of yourself, so stupid.

'It's working,' Jordan calls from the living room.

'Thank you,' she calls back.

'Can you just leave me alone now? Just leave me alone!' he yells and then she hears the slam of his bedroom door and she is suddenly exhausted. Her body sags against the kitchen counter. There is still so much to do but what she would really like to do is just curl up and go to sleep.

She walks back into the living room, where Jordan has left

the television on and all the plastic packaging on the floor. He could have cleaned up. As she bends down to pick up the plastic and find the instruction manual for the television, she tries to suppress the wave of dislike she feels for her son.

It's not something she would ever share with anyone because this is her fault, her and Mike's fault. Jordan is the product of the life she has helped build. He is the product of the man she chose to have children with. But sometimes she just doesn't like her child. It's an awful thought.

Who will he grow up to be, this angry child? If she had left sooner, would he be different? And because she has left now, who will he become?

She returns to the kitchen and lifts up her phone to text Paula but then drops it back onto the laminate kitchen counter. There's no real point. She knows what her sister would say because she's been saying it for the last few months, ever since Amanda told her the truth and then told her what she was going to do.

You're doing the right thing. You'll be fine. You're stronger than you know. You've got this. I will come over if you need me to. You're going to be fine. The kids will be fine. And you don't have to be there forever. But you need to be there now.

She needs to keep going with her unpacking because soon the kids will want dinner and she hasn't even made her bed or the children's beds yet, something she really should have done first.

As she collapses one of the packing boxes, another flash of a memory assaults her, something she dismissed at the time and then pushed to the back of her mind.

Twelve years ago, when she and Mike got married after his divorce from Annette was finalised and her parents had given their reluctant blessing, she was giddy with joy, desperate to start a family and be a real wife to Mike. The day before the wedding, she was looking through all the beautiful gifts they had already received when she found an unopened envelope.

It wasn't attached to a gift and so she opened it, expecting it to be a cheque, but it was just a card, a picture of a beautifully decorated white wedding cake on the front and a few words from her husband's ex-wife inside.

I hope he's what you want. Be careful.

Annette.

Now she recalls laughing and tearing up the card before throwing it away because she didn't want Mike to see it. *Jealous old witch,* she thought.

She should have paid attention to those words.

FOUR

Jordan

This is the most disgusting bedroom I have ever been in. The walls look dirty and there's some kind of weird smell. I can't believe I'm here. I can't believe she did this. I can't believe she thinks she can get away with this.

The only thing I was looking forward to in my whole shitty life was getting a gaming computer, my first actual computer and not one that the whole family can use. Dad told me that he was getting me one when he got back from China and now that's all screwed.

I'm sitting on the floor, waiting for the game to load, and I have to hold on to my iPad with both hands so I don't throw it against the wall. I want to throw something, kick something, smash something. I want to scream in her face until she cries.

In our last week of term, we had some dickhead come in to talk about feelings and puberty and other shit we know already and he said that sometimes, feelings have colours and blah, blah. I didn't listen to most of the stuff he said because I was zoned out but he's right about feelings and colours. Inside me is a glistening red rage. It starts at my toes and goes all the way up to my brain, making me sweat.

I hate this house and this street and this suburb. I hate that she did this, that she moved us here, that she just packed up our stuff and made us get in the car. I hate her. I hate her. I hate her. Who does she think she is? How does she think she can get away with this? 'Bitch,' I whisper, liking the way the word sounds. 'Bitch, bitch, bitch.'

I click on the Discord messaging board and message my dad. It's so stupid that I don't have a phone. Everyone has a phone at my age. Her rules are stupid and he just let her make them.

Dad are u in China yet??

You need to contact me asap. mum's gone crazy and moved us out of the house.

Dad???? did you land yet???

Please. U have to come get us. U have to come get me. i can't live here. i want to go home.

Dad??

I look up the flight time to China, to Shanghai. Ten hours and fifteen minutes but he won't have his phone on for ages after that. Will he check Discord? Why would he? He has to. He has to check it and come home and get me out of here. He has to get me away from her. He hates her as well. I know he does. She's so uptight, so hard to live with. He just wants to be left alone like I do. Why can't she understand that? What is wrong with her?

I see the rage, the glistening red, see it filling up every part of me.

I lift the iPad to throw it, see it smashing against the wall and the glass cracking.

But then the screen lights up and the game is ready. I watch as players join and my brain lets go of everything else to concentrate on what I'm doing.

My character appears on screen. And now it's okay for a bit.

But she can't leave me alone for long. And after a shitty dinner she starts with me again.

'Jordan, the television won't download the apps, can you come and sort it out?'

I ignore her. Let her sort out the stupid television, let her make things work. She's the one who screwed it all up.

'Jordan!' she shouts.

'Leave me alone!' I scream back.

She pushes open my door, and I hate her so much, I want to throw the iPad at her. 'You need to help me, Jordan.'

'No, I hate you, I hate it here. I hate this house. Why can't you just leave me alone? Just leave me alone.' I can feel the anger making me hot. I'm burning with anger.

'Don't you scream at me like that, don't you dare yell. All I asked for was some help, just get off that bloody device now, Jordan.'

I bite down on my cheek so I don't say anything else. I have to get out of here. Grabbing my iPad and my backpack, I stand and shove past her to the front door. I have to get away from her, from here, from this house and this street.

I have to get away.

FIVE

Caroline

It's just after 8 p.m. so I decide it's a fine time to go over and welcome the new family to the cul-de-sac. I think they will have had enough time to get unpacked and it's still too early for them to have decided to go to bed. I feel sorry for a woman on her own because it's not easy to raise children by yourself but perhaps it is a choice that had to be made. I have known many such women who have made the decision to leave a bad marriage and I know that frequently, throughout my childhood, I wished my mother would make that choice. But she was trapped by her lack of education, her inability to get a job, society's expectations. I don't blame my mother for staying because sometimes it's the only possible option. Things are different now but many women still find themselves trapped in terrible situations.

I've put the cake in my second-best plastic cake container, picked up from a discount store, because you never know if a container will be returned, and if I never get this one back, I'll be fine.

It's still warm and light. I think January is the nicest time of the year. It's never as hot as February and it feels as if the balmy days may well go on forever. They won't, of course, everything good ends eventually.

'Where are you going?' I hear and I turn to see Gemma coming out of her house. I walk over to her, finding myself in two minds about the way she looks, as I usually do.

Gemma has lived on this street for eight years, but in the last two years, since she became a single mother, she has transformed herself. She used to be a rather skinny, mousy woman, who seemed almost afraid to look anyone in the eye. But then she changed, almost blossomed, and, to me, seemed to take things too far. The first thing she did was to colour her hair a startling white blonde that I know costs her a fortune to maintain, and then she had her breasts enlarged so that they now strain against anything she wears, huge and round. I also seem to remember her eyes being a light brown in colour but they are now bright blue so she is obviously wearing coloured contact lenses, which seems a waste if you ask me. She looks like a Barbie doll come to life. I worry she can't be setting a good example for her two daughters – Chloe, who is ten, and Jessa, who is twelve – but that is an opinion I keep to myself. Both her girls are away at some camp for the next three weeks, something that more and more Australian parents seem to be doing over the summer holidays. They are both keen gymnasts and Gemma is very proud of them. I'm sure they'll get along famously with the new little girl in the cul-de-sac.

Today Gemma is dressed in a pair of tiny denim shorts and a white singlet, her hair in a messy bun and a tiny designer clutch bag in her hand in the improbable shape of a penguin. Not a bag for a grown woman if you ask me.

'New neighbours,' I say, gesturing towards Cora's house and the large black car in the driveway.

'Do they have kids?'

'It's just her, I think, and she has two, a boy and a girl.'

'That will make mine happy if either of them are the same age.' She takes a lip gloss out of a tiny pocket in her shorts and expertly coats her lips in shimmering pink.

'Going out?'

She nods.

'It's very late and won't you be... cold?'

'I'm just getting picked up for a drink, Caroline, and it's only with a friend.'

'Not a date?'

Gemma focuses her deep blue eyes on my face. 'No,' she says, a small smile on her face, 'he's busy.'

I would love to ask her more about the mysterious 'he' but Gemma doesn't share any of that information with me. I'm not overly concerned since none of the 'hes' she dates ever last very long.

'I'm just having some fun tonight.'

I have many opinions on what should constitute 'fun' but I keep those to myself. Despite some things I disagree with about her behaviour, I like Gemma. She's not terribly smart but I know she works hard during the day running a make-up counter in a department store, something she has described as tedious but 'worth it for the free make-up'. And I know she is a very good mother in other ways, dedicated to her daughters. With them away at camp, at least they aren't seeing her go out like this.

A car with an Uber sign in the front window pulls up.

'Have a good night,' I say as she climbs into the car, and she waves, leaving me to get on with my mission to welcome the new neighbours.

As I approach the house, I can see that the curtains in the living room have been closed already, which is a shame since it's still light outside. And then I hear the yelling, so loud that I stop just before my feet hit the driveway, as I listen, unsure what to do.

'No, I hate you, I hate it here. I hate this house. Why can't you just leave me alone? Just leave me alone.' It's obviously the boy shouting. I can hear the wobbliness of a breaking voice in his vitriol-filled tone.

'Don't you scream at me like that, don't you dare yell. All I asked for was some help, just get off that bloody device now, Jordan,' his mother screams back and I shake my head.

It's never a good idea to scream back at your child, it only makes them aware that they've made you lose control. I was always so careful with Janine. When she would go through her teenage rages, instead of matching her anger and frustration with my own, I would become calmer and quieter. It always worked and her tantrums soon petered out.

I wait for a moment, wondering exactly what I should do because it does not seem to be a good time to deliver a cake. On the other hand, a cake might be just what's needed, something sweet and delicious to distract everyone. I'm sure they're all just tired and cranky. Moving is a lot of work, especially for a woman on her own.

Before I can make any decision one way or another, the front door opens and the boy comes stomping out, his face a thundercloud of anger and his cap on backwards. He is carrying a backpack over one shoulder.

'Bitch,' he shouts into the air and then he sees me and stops. 'What are you looking at?' he spits and I am so shocked I have no idea what to say.

'Jordan, come back here,' I hear her shout from inside the house.

'I'm going to the park, just let me go,' he yells back, his gaze focused on me as though daring me to say anything.

I know that this generation have not been raised with the

same values as previous generations but it's rare to find a child who will be so obviously rude to an older person.

He stalks off up the street. I expect that at any moment his mother will come running out after him to stop him. Despite his height, his skin is still smooth so I can't imagine he is much older than eleven or twelve, far too young to be allowed to simply go off on his own at this time of night if you ask me, but obviously no one has asked me.

There is silence from inside. Perhaps she is glad to have some respite from the child. I do remember those moments as a mother as well.

I dither in the driveway for a minute as the boy disappears around the corner and then I push my shoulders back and march over to the front door, knocking with three short raps and stepping back a bit so that if the new resident is not ready for company, I can simply thrust the cake at her, say 'welcome to West Street' and leave.

'You'd better be ready to—' I hear and the door is flung open by the mother of the child, fury etched on her face as well. 'Oh,' she says when she sees me, and I watch as her shoulders drop. She peers past me, looking up the street.

'I'm so sorry. I thought...' She waves her hand, 'never mind,' and offers me a smile. She has one of those faces that is changed with a smile, and I cannot help but smile back. I can see she is tired from the shadows underneath her brown eyes. I am sure it's been a very long day. She smooths back her highlighted brown hair, tucking a few loose strands behind her ear.

'I saw your son leave.'

'Sorry about my son,' she says at the same time. 'He... he's going to the park. It looks safe and it's nearby.'

She peers out at the street as though she will be able to see the park, which I do know myself is very nice for the neighbourhood. It's just been redone with rubber matting, lots of play equipment and plenty of open space for walking.

'He'll be fine, he'll come home when his iPad runs out of battery,' she adds and then she looks at me again, making me feel quite silly for standing here, holding a cake.

'My name is Caroline and I live over the road. I saw you arrive this morning and I thought, well... Welcome! I hope you'll be happy here,' I say, thrusting the cake at her, regretting my decision now. The woman is obviously not up for company.

'Oh,' she says, looking down at the cake which I must admit has turned out really well. I have added the word 'welcome' in fresh cream on top of the double layer cake. I am very pleased with my efforts. It was so nice to have something concrete to do today. It seems to me that my life gets emptier every month, something I could not conceive of when Janine was little or when Liam was sick and I was caring for him. But I have jars and jars of pickled vegetables in the basement already and next Christmas is very far away. My knitting keeps me busy and I have good friends, good neighbours. It would be nice to welcome this new woman to our friendship group but I'm not sure about her yet. I need to get to know her much better before I invite her into our little trio. Mary, Gemma and I know a lot about each other and we trust each other so I would not want someone who we couldn't trust. But that's why I'm here.

'I'm Amanda. Please come in and please excuse the mess. I have a long way to go.'

I follow her inside to the living room, where boxes are everywhere, most of them opened, paper spilling out. Bubble-wrapped plates are sitting on the coffee table alongside some pale blue platters from a dinner service. It's not for me to say but I would have begun with the most important boxes and finished those before moving on to the next ones, but perhaps she has done this. I shouldn't rush to judge her.

'This is so lovely of you,' she says, 'I could use something sweet. Would you like a cup of tea?'

I would very much like a cup of tea but I can tell that

Amanda would be thrown out by this today. Who knows if she has even thought to unpack the kettle.

'No, I can see you have your hands full but it would be lovely to chat another day. Is it just you and your son?' I know the answer but she is not to know that I was watching her when she arrived.

Amanda leans down to the coffee table and pushes some things along, putting the cake container down.

'Me and my two children. Jordan, who you saw, is eleven, and Kiera is nine. She's in her room at the moment, practising standing on her head.' She smiles.

'I could never imagine doing that,' I say. 'And your husband is...?' I try to appear casual.

'We're separated.' Her reply is quick and abrupt but I can hear the pain behind the two-word sentence.

'I am sorry.'

'Do you have children?' she asks politely, changing the subject.

'I have a daughter but she lives in Melbourne. She's married but, so far, no grandchildren.' I shrug. Even if Janine has a child one day, I am unsure how much I would get to see him or her. My daughter and her husband are very busy people and I don't like to fly. There is something strange about being up so high in the air that bothers me. And there is the possible issue of her not wanting me to meet her child, a thought that I instantly dismiss. I would be a wonderful grandmother.

'And where did you come from?' I ask. 'Far away or have you moved from somewhere close?'

'Um...' A flush spreads across her face again. 'Over an hour from here.'

I wait for her to name the suburb she has come from but when she doesn't, I decide it's time to leave.

'Well, I just wanted to welcome you. I hope you'll be very happy here. It's a lovely neighbourhood and very safe. I know your son is out but you don't have to worry about him at all. Everyone is very nice.'

'Thank you. I'm sure he'll be back soon; he just went to explore, really, and he's pretty good at figuring out where he is. He knows to be home by the time it gets dark.'

'Well, I should be going, but I'm across the road if you need anything at all, any help or anything. I live alone and I have time on my hands,' I smile, waving my hands at her, 'so please don't hesitate to ask.'

'Thank you so much,' she says, walking me to the front door. 'I'm looking forward to meeting all the neighbours.'

We step outside, where the air is still warm but darkness is rapidly descending. I look up the street but there is no sign of her son.

'Thank you again.' She bites down on her lip and I know her thoughts have returned to where her child might be.

'My pleasure,' I reply and then she steps back inside and closes the door.

Poor woman. She is perhaps a little older than Janine, but not by much.

Thinking about my daughter always brings back the last conversation we had, the last time we spoke to each other.

It was the day of Liam's funeral. We had a wake in our local pub and all day she had been there, not next to me but talking to people, making sure everyone had enough to eat and drink.

'At least you have Janine to comfort you,' many people said, or versions of that, and I nodded and smiled even though I knew that she was angry at me.

But when everyone was gone, when the bill had been paid and I was walking back to my car, exhausted and sad, she came up to me.

'Are you coming back to the house?' I asked her and she shook her head.

I remember staring at my daughter for a moment, all the

things I wanted to say to her crowding into my mind. There was so much she didn't know, so much she refused to acknowledge. But I couldn't find a way to say anything at all.

Instead, I shrugged and got into my car, opening the window so I could say goodbye to her.

But I never got to say anything and now, as I open my front door, her words come back to me. Her last cruel words before she turned away. 'I know what you did,' she told me, her voice soft in the late-afternoon sunshine. 'And I will never forgive you.'

SIX

Amanda

As soon as she shuts the door on Caroline, she checks her watch. How long has Jordan been gone?

Five minutes? Maybe ten.

She picks up the cake and takes it to the kitchen.

'Kiera,' she calls, 'come and see.'

'Who gave you that?' asks Kiera, her eyes wide with delight, when she comes into the kitchen and sees the cake that Amanda has taken out of the container and put on a plate.

'Caroline, the lady from across the road, isn't that nice?'

Kiera nods her head and climbs onto a chair. 'Can I have a piece now, right now?'

Kiera is supposed to have her shower soon and Amanda doesn't usually allow treats so late at night but she can see no reason to say no. She cuts both herself and Kiera a generous slice each and they sit at the kitchen table piled with plates and cups still waiting to be put away.

The cake is delicious, the rich chocolate balanced perfectly by the fresh cream, but Amanda can only focus on the time passing. He's been gone for twenty minutes. He's been gone for thirty minutes. How safe is this neighbourhood? She should have stopped him.

'Shower time,' she tells Kiera when her daughter is done with her slice of cake.

'Where's Jordan? He loves chocolate cake.'

'He went for a walk. Go and shower so that he can shower when he gets back.' At home each child has their own en suite bathroom. Here, there is one for them to share and a tiny en suite for Amanda. *This is home now. How can this be home?*

There is more to do but she can only watch the time passing. He's been gone for forty minutes, now fifty. This is ridiculous. She can't just leave him out there. Kiera will have to come out in her pyjamas. She gets up from her chair and goes to find her shoes when there's a sharp rapping at the door.

Relieved, she flings it open. 'Jordan, thank God,' she sighs. He shrugs.

'Are you hungry?' she asks him instead of launching into the lecture she has had running through her head on repeat since the moment he left. He's always hungry these days.

He nods and then follows her to the kitchen, where she cuts him a large slice of the chocolate cake. She sits with him in silence as he wolfs it down in a few bites.

'Do you want another one?'

'No,' he says, standing up.

'Jordan, listen—'

'No,' he repeats and he leaves the kitchen.

She wants to cry but she collects herself and finishes her tea before unpacking a few more boxes and falling into bed. Tears are for the shower and are of no help right now.

The next morning, she waits until Jordan has woken up and then she sits both children down and tries to explain.

'Daddy and I can't live together anymore and be happy. We fight and yell and it's not good for anyone. But you will see your father as soon as possible. Nothing changes how much we both love you and you will see him as much as you want to.'

'I didn't like the yelling,' Kiera says. Amanda smiles at her, knowing that her daughter is showing her support.

'I don't want to live with you. I want to live with Dad,' her son states and then he gets up and leaves, returning to his room and his iPad. He is shutting her out at every opportunity.

Ten minutes later he comes out with his backpack over his shoulder. 'I'm going to the park.'

'No, you need to unpack your boxes first.'

'I'm. Going. To. The. Park.'

'Jordan, I said—'

'Leave me alone,' he thunders and he goes to the front door, pulling it open as she follows him.

He starts running so she can't stop him but he doesn't notice an old woman and her walker and he barrels right into her, nearly knocking her over.

Amanda rushes out as Jordan takes off up the street. 'I'm so sorry, so sorry,' she says, touching the frame of the walker as the woman stares at her with faded green eyes.

'He's in a hurry, isn't he?'

'He's just... I am sorry, are you hurt?'

'No, no, I'll be fine.' The woman straightens up. She's wearing a black cardigan, despite the heat. 'But now that you're here, I did want to ask if it would be possible to ask him, your boy, not to yell so much at night. It did make it very hard to sleep last night.'

'Oh dear, I am so sorry.' Amanda feels herself grow hot with embarrassment. 'I'll definitely talk to him. Are you sure you're all right?'

'Been through worse,' the woman mutters.

Across the street, the door of the house where Caroline lives opens and she appears, walking over to them. 'Oh, you two have met.'

'Not been formally introduced,' says the old woman.

'This is Mary,' says Caroline, 'she lives next door to you.'

'I'm Amanda,' she says with a quick smile, desperate to go back inside.

'Yes, well, I'd best get back,' says Mary and she turns, making slow, laborious progress back to her house.

'I think I upset her. She says Jordan kept her awake last night,' says Amanda.

'Oh, no... I'm sure it's fine. She's lovely and she'll be a great friend once you get to know her. We're all good friends here in this street so please don't hesitate to ask for help from anyone,' says Caroline.

'I will and thank you, and the cake was lovely, I'll get your container back to you.'

'Oh, no need to rush. I'm so glad you enjoyed it.'

'I do need to... to... get back but thank you again for the cake.' Amanda turns to go back inside.

'Maybe we could all have tea one day,' says Caroline and Amanda stops and turns back.

'Yes, that would be lovely, when I'm a bit more... settled.'

'Good, you'll meet Gemma soon, I'm sure. She's close to your age. You should get along famously.'

Amanda nods and then goes back into her house, shutting the door gratefully behind her.

She has no desire to meet anyone else and have them judge her and her family but Caroline seems determined to make them all friends. It seems that the cake was more than just a sweet welcome gift.

It was an attempt to gather information, to evaluate the new residents. It was Caroline's way in, but Amanda is not really interested in making friends.

She's interested in surviving.

SEVEN

Caroline

I don't think it's going to be that easy to get to know the new neighbour. She seems to want to keep to herself but I am determined to know more about her.

On my morning walk, I notice that her car is missing, which means she's obviously off at the shops or doing something else.

I walk over to the house, taking in the front garden, which definitely needs some water.

I can see that the mailbox is full and I step forward, opening the front, peering inside. She only arrived a few days ago so there's unlikely to be anything for her, but perhaps she's received some mail here already.

I search the street quickly but there are no signs of her returning so I bend down and pull out a whole lot of advertising pamphlets, rifling through them quickly.

And then I notice a large envelope at the back that looks quite official. It could be for Cora, I suppose, but I'm sure her son has redirected all her mail. As I'm moving in to grab the envelope, I hear the purr of a car behind me and I jump, shutting the mailbox, the pamphlets still in my hand. I quickly shove them back into the box, hoping that she doesn't check the mail today. I will return tonight for a bit more snooping.

I step aside as Amanda's car pulls into the driveway, my heart thumping in my chest as I hope she hasn't seen me.

When she has switched off her car, she opens her door and steps out and I brace myself for questions.

'Oh, Caroline, I'm so glad I caught you,' she says. 'Let me just go and get your container.'

'Oh... no need, no rush, I was just off on my walk.'

'Can I just leave it on your front step?'

'Yes, yes,' I say, feeling a light sheen of sweat on my face. I really just want to be away from her. 'I just need to walk before it gets too hot.' I don't think she saw me, and if she did, she's covering it very well.

'Good idea,' she replies and she goes to her boot, opening it up and taking some parcels out. I wave and move off quickly, leaving her to her unpacking.

She seems so nice, so friendly but only to a point. Why?

I'm sure this young woman is hiding something and I want to know what it is.

And I have a feeling the envelope might be a good place to start unravelling the truth about her.

EIGHT

Amanda

The next few days are more difficult than Amanda could have imagined.

Jordan seems to get worse every day, angrier and more aggressive and demanding that he be allowed to go home. 'This is not my home,' he screams at her one night when they have been in the house for nearly a week. 'I don't want to be here. I don't want to be with you. I want to be with Dad, you're not allowed to just take kids away from their fathers, it's illegal.'

'I'm not taking you away,' she replies, trying to keep her voice down in the hope that he will lower his as well, because she knows that all the shouting is bothering Mary. The woman has politely complained every single day. She seems to lurk in the garden, just waiting for Amanda to come out and hang the washing so she can speak to her.

'You may not know this yet but it's very hard for an older person to sleep anyway. To be disturbed is bad for my health,' she said yesterday as Amanda hung washing quickly, apologising for her son again.

She has asked Jordan to keep the noise down, to whisper or just talk instead of shout, and he seems to understand but he only lowers his voice for a short time before the shouting starts again. Kiera sleeps through anything and Amanda is so tired that she's able to simply block out the noise.

She has thought about punishing Jordan for his behaviour by taking away the iPad and banning gaming on the television and she has threatened to do this more than once. But Jordan knows she won't. She has a feeling that Jordan knows she is just a little afraid of him.

'I'm not taking you away,' she repeats. 'You will see your father as soon as possible, I promise you,' she tells him, as he looks at her with his lip curled and dislike etched across his face.

As soon as he's agreed to a divorce, as soon as we have parenting orders in place, as soon as I stop being afraid that he will kill me.

'You're a lying bitch,' he spits at her and then he stomps off to his room, as she stands, tense and waiting for the furious slam of his bedroom door. Only then does she relax, knowing that she won't see him for the rest of the night.

To her shame, when the pizza arrives, she sends Kiera to get him and then she deliberately washes up at the sink with her back turned until he comes and grabs his pizza and leaves. Usually, she would cajole him to join them but she just wants some peace from him.

Getting into bed, a stray thought catches her, making her sick with the idea of it. *I have run from an abuser but brought one with me.*

This terrible truth compels her to spend hours scrolling through message boards on websites for mothers, reading other experiences with teenage boys as all the while the idea that he is not yet a teenager is foremost in her mind. She finally succumbs to sleep just after three in the morning when Jordan is quiet and she is completely drained.

. . .

And then it is Sunday morning, the Sunday morning she has been waiting for.

She has been waiting for the first message or call from Mike that she knew would come today, her body tensed, even in sleep, with the fear of it coming.

But her late-night scrolling means she is asleep when it arrives, instead of prepared.

It starts with two words, just after 10 a.m., just after he would have walked into his office, fresh from his flight in business class and a week of schmoozing with suppliers who take him out to expensive dinners.

The sound of the alert drags her from a deep sleep and she grabs her phone, rubbing her eyes to see clearly.

YOU BITCH

She stares at the words, and is surprised to feel not the terrible panicked waiting she has felt all week but rather a detached calm.

Mike is back and it has begun.

It's over. He knows.

She doesn't reply because she's read all the articles, listened to the podcasts, watched the videos. She knows not to reply, not to acknowledge what he has said. She will let him say everything he wants to say, let him rant over text, let him become aware that she will not be baited into a hasty reply, and then she will send him her answer. These are just words, and while words hurt, they don't break the skin, don't snap a bone. She will deal with the words.

She gets out of bed and takes a shower, keeping the phone close, not wanting Kiera or Jordan to somehow see the message. She is not letting the phone out of her sight anyway, fearful that

Jordan will try and call his father. She's even changed the lock pattern to one only she knows and she feels terrible about this subterfuge but she has no choice. She dresses and then she goes to make herself a coffee, all the time admiring herself for her calm, her ease, her numbness.

Twenty minutes later, the exact amount of time it would take Mike to get from his store to their house, there is another message.

You will regret this. I promise you faithfully that you will regret this.

And her wall of detachment crumbles and panic floods through her body, making her sweat in the warm kitchen. Words can invoke fear and panic. Words speed up the heart rate. Perhaps words can kill you. Her hands tremble as she takes her first sip of coffee.

He won't find us, she reminds herself because she has deleted the tracking app from her phone. He likes to know where she is at all times, but now he won't be able to find her. She has deleted the app from the children's iPads as well. They are everywhere and nowhere.

Please God, don't let him find us.

She understands his anger. He has walked into their house and found it empty of her clothes, empty of the children's belongings, empty of the kitchen stuff but still full of the beautiful furniture she chose so carefully. The furniture he indulgently paid for with only a wry smile because she told him exactly why she loved and needed each piece.

He must be nearly apoplectic with anger.

She can see him in his casual grey chinos and black button-down shirt, his usual travelling outfit, can see him pacing through the rooms, taking note of everything that has been taken. Her empty closet will bother him the most, all those designer handbags and all that jewellery he gave her, gone. She is keeping it safe here, because she knows she will need to sell more of it. Mike kept her on a tight leash with money. She has an account he put money into, but only so much and no more.

He bought the gifts for the kids, he paid the bills and the mortgage, he bought her designer clothes and bags. She bought groceries. Every charge on her credit card was queried so she had to keep a folder filled with receipts ready for him to peruse every month. There's no way she will use the card now in case it gives away her location. Financial abuse is what it's called now, but when it began, when they were first married, it made sense. She didn't work because she was pregnant soon after they got married and that was always the plan. She didn't earn the money and so it was only fair that he got to decide how it should be spent. That's how she explained it to herself.

She opens up another text message on her phone.

You don't know me but...

She doesn't read the rest of it because she knows it by heart. This is all she has to fight back with, just this message, and she hopes that no one ever sees it but her. She hopes she will not need to use it.

She takes another sip of coffee but finds it difficult to swallow, a large lump appearing in her throat so the liquid hurts going down.

Mike will find them soon enough. He's a clever man and will ask the neighbours questions and then he will find the moving company and then he will know where they are. Will she be ready for him when he gets here? Can a person actually be ready for this?

The children will be here. He will behave in front of the children lest the good guy image become tarnished. He is the children's hero. He is the good guy that the whole neighbourhood likes. He never raises his voice to them, certainly never uses physical punishment, and often, very often, will cajole her on their behalf into giving in on rules she has in place.

But soon the children will start school and she will be alone for many hours in the day. Shaking her head as she makes herself another cup of coffee, she examines some of her more magical thinking this week. She imagined, in a best-case scenario, that he would be incensed but mostly that he would be shocked by what she has done. She threatened to leave him eleven times. And each time she wrote it down in a notebook so she could see that she had made the threat, hoping that the written words would make her keep her promise.

But each time, she chickened out, was simply waiting for him at home when he returned from work, dinner on the table and her self-loathing more extreme.

But this time, she didn't threaten. This time she didn't say a word, instead just writing the words down for herself as she made her plans. He will struggle to believe she's had the guts to do it.

And because of that, she imagined that when he did find them, they would be able to have a civil conversation from the other side of the screen door. The lockable screen door at the front was important to her, her repeated questions about it confusing the real estate agent. She thought that maybe, just maybe, she could get him to agree to mediation and to agree that they need to separate and move on with their lives. That was a fantasy, a silly fantasy.

You know there's no way I won't find you, right? I will find you.

'I know you will,' she says aloud.

As she has done over the past week more than once, she considers calling the police, something that Paula has suggested she do. 'Have them there when he comes and then he'll know not to put a foot wrong.'

But when will he be here? Can she call the police and say that at some point he will turn up?

You think you've won something here? You've won nothing and you're going to regret this. I told you that if you ever left me, you would regret it.

Will Mike find them today? Tomorrow? How long do they have? And what might he do when he finds them? Sometimes in an argument, behind the closed door of their bedroom when he hurt her in a particular way, she would say, 'You don't deserve to be a father. You don't deserve a family,' even knowing that more pain was coming because she dared to say the words.

Once when she said it, he grabbed her arm and twisted it behind her back, lifting it higher and higher until she knew that just one more movement would dislocate it. As the shock of the pain spread through her body, he whispered into her ear, 'They are my children and I get to decide what they deserve. Maybe you don't deserve to be a mother and I promise you, Amanda, I can make that happen.'

The next day, the apology flowers were an extra-large bouquet, accompanied by a note: *I hate when we fight and you make me say things that I regret xxx*

There will be no civil mediation. She can see that now but she is still holding on to some hope, some small hope that now that he knows other people are involved because she has a lawyer, he will back down, back off, accept it.

But he won't. If she doesn't do as he says, he will drag her back to her marriage, and then it's very likely that he will kill her. But she can't give up now. Not after everything she has done to get this far.

In the years since the abuse began, she has often thought

about contacting Annette, Mike's first wife. She lives in the UK now but was easy enough for Amanda to find on Instagram, where she posts pictures of her walks with her dog. Amanda has begun a message to Annette at least ten times, asking her why she didn't warn Amanda properly, why she didn't explicitly state the reality of who Mike was. She has wanted to ask the older woman how long it took her to learn the truth about Mike and why she stayed as long as she did – or had she been trying to leave for years? But each time she has been on the verge of sending the message, she has deleted it. Humiliation over her own choices has kept her from contacting the woman whose husband she slept with, fearing that Annette would reply with something like, *You got yourself into this*.

Because Amanda did get herself into this and so she probably wouldn't have listened to any kind of warning anyway. Her parents gave their blessing but they cautioned her about the age difference between her and Mike and about how quiet she became around him, even at her own family dinners. Amanda brushed off their opinions, her love for Mike all-consuming. And now she is here and she knows that she needs to get herself out of this. *And I will do that. I am doing that.*

With trembling fingers, she sends the text she has composed and written and rewritten at least twenty times.

> ***I understand you're angry and I'm sorry about that. But you and I both know we can't continue on as before. I want a divorce and I will get one. Once you agree, you will be able to see the children as much as you like. My lawyer's name is on the papers and if you call her, she can arrange a meeting for the two of us in her office. You know why I have to leave. I need to protect myself. I'm begging you to just make this as easy as possible***

so we can both move on with our lives. I'm sure you will find someone who is right for you.

She's very sure about that.

You don't get to leave me and survive it, Amanda. You just don't. If you come home now, we can just move on. We'll have dinner and laugh about it. But you have one chance to get back here.

You cannot threaten me. This is a threat and I will report it to the police.

Go right ahead.

She stares down at the words, stunned by his arrogance, by his confidence. He doesn't care. Why doesn't he care?

Leaving the kitchen, she takes the phone into the back garden, where the grass is green and neatly trimmed after a visit from a gardening company. As she steps outside, she hears the front door slam and she's ashamed of how relieved she is.

Jordan has gone to the park again and the tension that shimmers in the air when he's here has gone along with him.

And he's not here to hear her make this call.

She needs to do this now. Quickly, before Kiera can come outside and find her and ask what they are doing today, she looks up the number for the local police station and taps on it, glancing around to see if Mary is already in her back garden.

'Delmont police station,' answers a man, his voice a low rumble.

'Yes, hi, hello, um... Look, I don't know how to do this... or what to... but I've left my husband and I've moved away and now he's going to come and find me.' She feels so stupid as she stumbles over her words.

'Right,' says the man and she can hear that she hasn't actually explained anything to him.

Squeezing the cup of coffee in her hand, she tries to focus her thoughts. 'He's um, so he was away and now he's back, and while he was away, I packed up the kids and moved and left him divorce papers. And now he's going to find me but he's angry and he told me that I don't get to leave him and survive it.' She stops speaking, leaving Mike's threat hanging in the air.

'And has he ever been violent with you or the children?'

Amanda takes a sip of her coffee, buying herself some time.

If she tells this policeman that Mike has hurt her, he will want to know why she hasn't reported it and it will be her fault. She can feel that it will be her fault because it is her fault. She should have left the first time it happened when Jordan was a baby. That's what she should have done. But it was just once and he was so sorry and he absolutely promised that it would never, never happen again.

She has no actual proof, no photos, no record of anything he has done. It was their secret and it was meant to stay that way. It was something that only happened in their bedroom, only after the children were definitely asleep. The fighting, the use of ugly words – that went on in front of them. But the punches, the hair pulling, the twisting of her arm behind her back, the slapping... that went on in their bedroom, in front of the king-sized timber sleigh bed with luxurious dark blue bamboo linen. For eleven years it has been their little secret, sick and twisted but something that almost bonded them together.

Mike is a good guy, generous with money for charity, adoring of his children, helpful in the neighbourhood. But he has these moments with her, moments she accepted until she decided she couldn't do that anymore. She doesn't feel able to share this with a stranger on the phone.

'Not... really,' she says to the policeman.

'Right.' She can hear he doesn't believe her and she's

grateful for that. She wonders, briefly, how many other women have called police stations this week, how many others have said words similar to hers, how many others are afraid. One woman dies each week at the hands of her domestic partner in Australia. Isn't that the statistic?

'Does he threaten you with violence?'

'Yes.' Just living with Mike is a threat every day as she waits for him to cycle through contrite Mike to loving Mike to tense Mike to abusive Mike. 'And now he's threatened me again. I mean that's a threat, right?'

'It does sound like one, yes, and he is not allowed to get away with doing that.'

'Okay,' she says, swallowing, relieved that this is the case. 'Okay.'

'Does he control you in any way, as in financially or by tracking you?'

'He made me keep my location app on all the time but I've deleted that. He... he makes the money and he gave me money to run the house but he pays most of the bills, all of the bills.' She lifts her coffee cup to her lips but it's empty. She needs to eat something but she doesn't want to go back inside until she's done with this conversation.

'Do you have parenting orders in place?'

'No, I just took the kids and left. We haven't actually started the process yes.'

'And do you know where he is now?'

'I don't but he got back from his trip and I think he's going to come over here and I'm scared. But I'm not sure if he knows where we are, not yet.'

'Well, we take this matter very seriously. If he does come to your house and you or your children feel threatened in any way, then please call triple zero and an officer will attend the house immediately. I have your number here and you can give me your name and address as well.'

Amanda recites the address, making a mistake the first time.

'I suggest you take out an apprehended violence order with the court to prevent him coming near you as you navigate this process.'

'But can't you just come over and... wait?' *Idiot*. What did she think was going to happen, that they would just send over someone to wait with her like a bodyguard?

The officer takes a breath and then another breath, as though he has thought better of what he's about to say.

'If your husband turns up at the property and threatens you or the children, a police officer will attend immediately. Until he actually does something, we can't really get involved. If you have proof of any violence against you or your children, that would help.'

'No, no proof,' says Amanda, regretting not wanting to take pictures of her bruises because she was so shamed by them. The bruise she arrived here with has faded to a slight discolouration on her skin. It would be proof of nothing.

'I can send someone out to speak to him at your original address but then we will be required to let him know where his children are, unless you want to press charges, but in order to do that you need—'

'Proof.' She can feel humiliating tears in her eyes.

'I'm sorry, but an officer will get there in minutes if you call.'

'Okay, okay.' It's time to give this up. 'Thank you,' she says and she hangs up the phone with the words 'court order' and 'triple zero' playing on a loop in her head. When he comes here, will she have time to call triple zero? How on earth does she get an apprehended violence order? She should have asked her lawyer but she didn't tell her lawyer everything, just asked her to put irreconcilable differences down as a reason for the divorce. She wanted to make things as civil as possible, as easy as possible. A ridiculous idea.

Inside the house, Kiera is sitting at the dining room table, her craft supplies spread everywhere.

Amanda thought she was ready for this. A week ago, she thought she was ready but now she's not so sure.

'See, Mum,' says Kiera, holding up a card covered in glitter, 'it's for Jordan's birthday next month.'

Amanda smiles down at her daughter and reminds herself of the final straw, the terrible catalyst for this.

A few months ago, Kiera had been crying about something, and Amanda can't even remember what it was but Mike was home, and while Amanda had been trying to placate her normally happy child, Mike was just staring at her. They were in the kitchen and Mike was having a coffee before leaving for work, and he stood up and said, 'Kiera, you're making too much noise for a girl,' and then he looked at Amanda and said, 'and no one likes that,' with a smile and she knew, she just knew.

Mike never disciplined the children, was always their best friend, but they wouldn't be children forever. Kiera was going to grow up and turn into a teenage girl with her own opinions and probably some attitude. And Mike was not having that.

Another text comes through

Watch out, Amanda. I'm coming for you and I will take away everything you love.

She is not ready for this. Not at all.

NINE

Jordan

In the park, I watch all the little kids on the play equipment. They all seem so happy as they sit in swings or crawl over the climbing frame. Was I that happy? I can't remember. I can't remember being happy. If I look at old pictures of me, I seem happy but I can't remember it. And now there's just the glistening red anger, all the time, the anger.

Maybe these kids come from happy families where their mums are kind and nice and their dads don't need to yell. She makes him mad for no reason and then he yells and she yells back. But parents yell. When I used to go over to my friend Luke's house, I heard his parents yell at each other over stupid stuff like loading the dishwasher, but after the yelling, they would just be talking again like everything was fine. I think that bad stuff comes after the yelling with my parents. I think of the sounds I hear at night when they believe I'm asleep or they think I can't hear them because I'm gaming with my headphones on. I look over at the merry-go-round where some little kid is screaming for her mum. I concentrate on how that sound makes me crazy so that I don't have to think about the other sounds I've heard late at night in my house.

She makes him crazy. He always tells me that. He says, 'Your mother drives me crazy,' and I think, *Why can't she just stop? Just stop and then everything would be okay.* But now we're here and I can't stay here. I can't live here.

The park has free Wi-Fi and that's why I spend every day here. I log on to Discord and message him. I don't know why he hasn't replied.

> *I know U were only going away for a week. are U back now? can you come and get us?*

He's home. I know he's home.

> *Dad, are U there??? I hate this place. mum is being weird and the neighbours are all old and the wi-fi is shit and I have to spend all day in the park because the house smells and all mum does is ask me to help with stuff and I don't want to. can you just come and get me please and then you and mum can get a divorce and I can live with you. i won't make you mad like she did.*

I don't know why he won't reply. Is he angry with me as well? Does he think I knew what she was going to do?

> *dad, as soon as U see this U need to tell me. i can give you the address and everything. I won't tell mum if you come and get me. i'll just leave in the middle of the night and then she can be sorry for doing this.*

Maybe he's working. Maybe he doesn't want to see me? He must want to see me. Isn't he wondering where we are? Why hasn't he found us yet? He could if he wanted to. He can do anything he wants to do. One day, I'm going to be able to do whatever I want to. I'll live alone and it won't matter if they love me or hate me. I'll just be alone and I'll be fine. I wish I was eighteen. I wish I was already done with school. I wish I didn't feel so bad all the time.

Dad, why aren't you answering??? what's wrong with you? U need to come and get me. she shouldn't be allowed to pull this shit. i hate her. i hate it here.

'Is that an iPad?' I turn to see who's talking to me and it's some gross kid with ice cream on his face. I don't have money for ice cream. I don't have money for anything. Dad gives me money. He gives me money whenever I ask for it but she says she needs money for us to live. That's not my fault. I didn't run away from my home. I was forced to come here.

'Shut up, idiot,' I say and I shove him hard so he falls backwards. He starts crying.

'Hey,' shouts his mother, rushing towards me. I get up and run, leaving the park. Little kids are dumb. I used to be that dumb. I thought my mum loved me and wanted the best for me and only ever wanted to help me.

I'm not that dumb anymore.

TEN

Caroline

'It's the terrible disrespect I dislike,' I say, placing my cup of tea back on the saucer.

We are at Mary's house for afternoon tea. And we are discussing the new family, who I have really tried to like but cannot.

'It's awful,' agrees Mary. 'That child plays those video games all night and he seems to be playing with others online, which I know is something that happens because I've read about it, and he shouts and swears until all hours of the morning. It's all F this and F that and F you. Not appropriate language at all. I've had to ask her every day to tell him to keep it down because I need my rest. But I don't think she can tell him anything at all. She has no control of the child.'

'I haven't met her yet,' says Gemma, who has a day off and so has joined us for tea. There's a lot to discuss after all. 'But I've heard the shouting.'

'And,' continues Mary, 'she always says she will talk to him but then there is a look in her eyes, a kind of fear that I cannot believe. I remember when my James was an angry teenage boy. And it can be quite scary but the boy isn't even a teenager yet. She really should have better control.' Mary nods her head as she speaks, her indignation at the boy's behaviour blooming red in her cheeks.

'You shouldn't let it upset you so much,' I say.

'Well, the boy nearly killed me, didn't he?' She shakes her head, her hands trembling a little as she takes another sip of her tea. It's an exaggeration but Mary is frail and the world is a scarier place for frail people.

'How can it not upset me, Caroline? All I was doing was walking slowly past the house when their front door opened and the boy came storming out, yelling, "No, no, just stop telling me what to do," or whatever it is that he usually yells at her. And when I gave him one of my good stares, he pushed me.'

'He was just trying to get past you,' I say because I'm sure the boy didn't intentionally push her. I truly hope he didn't.

'Nonsense, and if he didn't mean to, why did she come running out filled with smiles and apologies?'

'It must have been very scary,' says Gemma, who is hearing the story for the first time. I have heard it many times already but I am trying to be patient.

'I have to get out and exercise as much as I can, doctor's orders.'

'Absolutely,' agrees Gemma, 'and you shouldn't be scared to go out or be pestered by the shouting in your own home.'

'That's right.'

'I worry about what will happen when my girls get home,' says Gemma. 'I mean, I'm sure they'll be going to the same school and they live right next to each other, what if he decides he doesn't like one of my daughters?'

'What if he decides that he does?' asks Mary, biting into a scone covered in jam and cream, leaving a whisper of cream on her upper lip. I hand her a serviette and she wipes her face.

We are silent as we all digest this little truth along with our ginger snap biscuits and scones.

'I can't remember what it was like to go to sleep without his shouting at his friends coming from next door. I don't know how she sleeps with it or why she lets it go on,' says Mary. 'If my James was here instead of overseas with his wife and children, he would soon sort her out.' Mary nods to a photograph on the mantelpiece of her husband and son, arms wrapped around each other, wide, slightly fake, smiles on their faces.

Gemma and I exchange a look.

'I think it may be time for me to try and talk to her,' I say because while I am sure that Mary has asked politely, I fear Amanda may need a more forceful approach.

'I wonder why she's left her husband?' asks Gemma.

'I have no idea. But it must be hard for her. It's always better if families stay together.'

'Not all families,' says Gemma darkly.

'Indeed,' I reply.

'Maybe if we knew more about her, we would be able to... I don't know, just let her know that we understand what she's going through. I mean... we know how hard it is to be a woman in the world today,' says Gemma, pouring herself another cup of tea from the pot.

Mary likes a proper pot of tea when the three of us are together and I do too. Gemma never eats any of the lovely things I make but then I suppose she has to fit into her tight skirts and tighter tops.

'Perhaps.' I judge this to be the moment to tell them what I know. I retrieve my bag and take an envelope out.

'What's that?' Gemma asks.

'Mail, from her mailbox.'

'I don't understand,' says Mary.

'Did you steal the woman's mail?' asks Gemma, a giggle escaping.

'Well... I was only checking the box because it was very full. I'll put it back tonight. I just wanted to know a bit more about her. I think we all do. Most of it was junk. Everything comes by email except,' I turn the envelope around to face them, 'school information packets. School starts soon, doesn't it, Gemma?'

Gemma nods as she and Mary stare at the envelope with the name of our local public school across it.

'What if she had caught you?' asks Mary, scandalised by what I have done.

'She nearly did the first time I tried, but if she had, I was going to tell her that Cora's son had asked me to check the mail for him.'

'Clever,' laughs Mary.

Gemma sits forward in her chair and grabs the envelope from me, peering down at the name. 'Amanda Caldwell,' she reads.

'Do you know her?'

Gemma shakes her head. 'It's a common name, I mean the surname, Caldwell. Last year Chloe had a boy in her class by that surname. It's very common,' she repeats.

'Well, we know her name now so can you find out anything else about her?' Gemma is a lot more internet savvy than me and Mary.

'We can find her... husband if we just... go on Instagram and Facebook and keep looking.' She swipes at the screen on her phone.

It takes only moments before she discovers Amanda's Facebook, which is private but has a picture of her whole family, including the husband, as a profile picture, and then an image search immediately identifies Michael Caldwell, owner of a very expensive jewellery store. 'Wow,' whispers Gemma. 'He's really good-looking. And he looks so... nice. We don't know exactly what's going on but maybe it's just an amicable divorce, two people separating to get on with their own lives.'

'Gemma, really,' I say at her mention of the man's looks. 'Maybe he's cut her off without a penny. Men do that. Why else would she be here in a house that will be knocked down in six months?'

'Not all men are terrible, Caroline,' says Gemma.

'Hmph,' says Mary.

'Well, now that we've found out who they are, what are we going to do with the information?' asks Gemma. 'We should really help her. I mean just be here to support her, especially if she's divorced or getting a divorce. It's better if you're out of an unhappy marriage and I know that it really helped me to have you here, Caroline, to support me when I needed someone to talk to.'

I'm not quite sure why Gemma has become quite so desperate to help Amanda all of a sudden but I nod my head in agreement. Women should help each other.

'Perhaps...' I am interrupted by shouting from next door and I sigh.

It's so loud they could be right here with us in the room.

'This is all your fault. The internet never goes out at home. I hate this shithole and I hate you.'

'It's not my fault,' she responds, 'I have nothing to do with it.'

'I don't want to be here. I hate you.' Such anger, such hate.

'Jordan, don't push me,' she screams and I stand because that cannot be allowed.

'Shut up, bitch, just shut up. I wish you were dead,' he shouts and then there is the thundering slam of the front door we have all grown used to over a single week.

'Well,' says Mary. 'What are you going to do now, Caroline?'

I turn to my two friends and shrug my shoulders because I am really not entirely sure, not sure at all. But I do know that we cannot live next door to this noise and chaos for the next six months. Mary is old and needs her sleep, and Gemma and I don't need awful neighbours to contend with. Gemma's little girls need to be safe in their own street. Both women are looking at me and I know they need me to make some sort of decision. We could report the noise to the police, perhaps even call the real estate agents and have them talk to her, but I still feel that if I could just talk to Amanda, she would welcome our help to deal with her child and our support as she goes through a divorce.

Something needs to be done because we do so value our peace here in the cul-de-sac. It's been hard won.

But do I have any right to interfere at all?

It's easy to suggest toying with people's lives, not so easy to deal with the consequences. I know that.

I study my two friends, wondering what the right thing to do is.

'I have to go.' Gemma stands, her face unusually pale.

'You should eat more, you know,' says Mary but Gemma waves her away and leaves, leaving the clean-up to me as usual.

'Off to meet another man, no doubt,' says Mary after she's left.

'She's young, Mary. Perhaps she doesn't want to be alone.'

'She has her girls like I have my James.'

I pick up the empty teapot to return it to Mary's kitchen.

On Mary's fridge is a Mother's Day card from James, store-bought with a picture of a vase of pink flowers on the front. She had him late in life after many years of trying. She lost three babies before he was born although lost is not quite the word – perhaps 'taken' is the better phrase. Three babies were taken from her by an angry fist to the stomach before she carried James to term.

Mary is fond of showing the card to me even though she knows I have seen it many times.

Inside it reads: *To the best mum ever. I hope next year is better. I love you. James xxxx.*

James was eighteen when he wrote that card, and it is the last one he ever gave her.

He's been dead for twenty-five years now but Mary needs the fantasy of him being alive.

The fantasy is all she has left.

ELEVEN

Amanda

As one day follows another, Amanda feels herself to be on the very edge of hysteria all the time. Mike has not sent another text but she can feel him getting closer to finding them, even without anything happening at all. She is familiar with this feeling of claustrophobic waiting, is familiar with it from the days when she knew that something was coming. It was never for any particular reason, but just because enough time had passed since the last time he'd hurt her, and she had learned to recognise his subtle searching for some reason to get angry. On those days, her breathing felt shallow, her heart rate quickened and she found herself unable to concentrate. On those days she paid extra attention to the house, making sure everything was in perfect order, making a lovely dinner, keeping the children quiet. She feels the same way now. But there is nothing she can do and she knows from experience that none of it worked anyway.

With each passing day she grows more frightened that this

will be the day he turns up, that he will be here soon. She is not sleeping, barely eating and snapping at the children

She and Jordan have fought every single day, sometimes two or three times a day, over everything from him unpacking his boxes to simply moving a plate from the dining room table to the sink. She feels like she's doing every single thing in the house. Perhaps that is simply what being a single mother is like. Maybe this is what she needs to get used to. She is exhausted, constantly sweaty, and she hates this little house and the ugly street and the neighbours who ask too many questions. When she chose to come here, her reasoning made sense but now she's not so sure.

Next door, Mary seems to wait in her back garden for Amanda to come outside so they can have a chat, which is mostly complaints about Jordan yelling at friends when he's gaming. And Caroline over the road is always hovering somewhere. Amanda is doing everything she can to avoid Gemma, who she has only seen from afar as she leaves for work or goes out at night. She looks, absurdly, like a plastic doll, and Amanda has no idea what she would even say to her.

She cannot imagine this being her life for six months or a year or however long it takes to sort out finances and custody and everything else surrounding two people pulling apart twelve years of marriage.

'Come on,' she exhorts herself now, 'you can do this.' She hauls herself out of bed to go and get some breakfast. The television that is usually on is not working because the Wi-Fi is out.

In the living room, Jordan and Kiera are sitting on the sofa playing pre-loaded games on their iPads. It's odd to see Jordan out of his room but the house doesn't have air conditioning and his room does get very hot.

'A technician is coming to fix the internet today,' she says by way of a greeting, 'so you will have Wi-Fi soon.'

'So what?' he sneers, without looking at her.

'Jordan, I know,' she begins, preparing to say the same things she has said for the last ten days.

He stands up and picks up his cereal bowl, walks over to her and stares down at her, and then he lifts his hand and points at her face. 'Shut up, just shut up. I don't want to hear it.'

Amanda steps back, her heart racing as she hears that his voice is lower than it was a week ago, sees that he has grown more over the last few days and understands that her eleven-year-old son is actually capable of hurting her, that he may actually want to hurt her. On Monday, he shoved her when she couldn't immediately fix the internet. And then he told her he wished she was dead.

'He didn't mean it, Mum,' Kiera said when she saw tears appear on her mother's face.

'I know, sweetheart, I know he didn't.' She hugged her daughter, holding her tight as she swallowed her distress.

Jordan had apologised when he came home, seeming to have shocked himself by his own behaviour. And she had imagined that things would be a bit easier for a few days, probably the same way she imagined that things would be easier for a few days after Mike hit her, and the juxtaposition of this had stunned her. But things are just as bad, worse even.

She hears him throw his cereal bowl in the sink, hears the sound of the bowl shattering, but she doesn't move until she hears his bedroom door open, and then while she stands, frozen, waiting, he walks through the living room and out the front door. The sound of it slamming sends a jolt through Amanda's body.

Who is this child? How is this the same sweet child who she gave birth to and fed and nurtured? At two he was all dimpled smiles and blue eyes, charming to everyone he met. At three and four and five he was a loving child who only wanted to be with his mum. She cannot remember when the change happened but she thinks it was sometime in the last year. At some point, he began looking at her the way Mike did sometimes, with disdain. And she was so busy trying to survive being married to Mike that she didn't address it and now he is this awful person and it's her fault and she doesn't know how to change it.

'Are we doing something fun today?' asks Kiera in a soft voice.

'Not today, sweetheart. I'm sorry but I need to clean up.' She is scared to leave the house, scared to stay in the house, and she doesn't have the energy for 'fun' and feels she may never have it again.

'This is not a happy place,' says Kiera and she gets off the sofa and walks away, closing her bedroom door behind her with a soft click. Her words are more devastating than Jordan's anger. Kiera has tried to be happy here. But it's impossible.

And suddenly she cannot stay where she is for one more minute. She needs to be out of here, out of this terrible house with her fuming child, and her sad but so sweet child. She wants to be away from all the mess and the chaos, just not here. If Mike turns up, she will be gone and the children can do what they want. She can't do this anymore, she just can't.

She grabs her keys and heads to her car, clicking the remote repeatedly, needing the door to be open so she can just speed away. But at the car she stops, resting her head against the door. She's not going anywhere, not leaving Kiera. Obviously not.

'Amanda,' she hears and she turns to find Caroline standing in the street. The older woman is wearing her usual outfit of capri pants and a loose shirt, her grey hair in a neat bob, and a string of blue beads around her neck.

Amanda takes a deep, shuddering breath. She cannot talk to anyone now, simply can't.

'Are you okay?' asks Caroline and Amanda wants to nod her

head but instead she shakes it and then the tears that she is supposed to save for the shower arrive.

In an instant, Caroline is next to her, an arm around Amanda's shoulders. 'There, there. It simply can't be all that bad, come, come with me and we'll have some tea at my house, come on.'

'Kiera is in the house,' gasps Amanda, 'I can't leave her.'

'All right then,' says Caroline firmly, 'now you take a deep breath and get a hold of yourself and I will get Kiera. I have a cat named Luna she will love. You can both come over and spend some time.'

Amanda nods her head because that sounds nice, it sounds relaxing, like anywhere but here.

Caroline goes into Amanda's house and is out with Kiera in a few minutes.

'Caroline has a cat,' says Kiera excitedly, 'and she has a garden with a bridge.'

Amanda has managed to stop her tears and has grabbed a tissue from the car to blow her nose. 'Won't that be fun,' she says with as much enthusiasm as she can muster, and Kiera nods.

Caroline leads them into her house where everything is neat and tidy and the air is filled with the smell of fresh cut roses.

'Sit down, sit here,' says Caroline, pulling out a chair next to a small square kitchen table, and Amanda drops into the chair, puts her bag and keys on her lap and tries to compose herself as Caroline introduces Kiera to her cat and then takes them both out into the garden. Amanda looks around the tidy kitchen, wishing her life was this under control.

'Now just let me take some of my chocolate chip cookies out to Kiera and we can have some alone time. I've asked her to keep the cat outside for a bit.'

Amanda nods, just happy to have someone else in charge for a few minutes. She can hear Kiera in the garden, talking to the cat as she walks around. The children would love a pet but Mike thinks that animals are disgusting.

I wish it wasn't his decision to make. One day it won't be.

Caroline puts a cup of tea in front of her and gently touches her on the shoulder.

She takes a sip of the tea that is hot but not too hot and then she picks up a cookie and devours it. Tears threaten again because no one has made her a cup of tea in years and it's so nice to have someone take care of her, even if just for a moment.

'Moving can be overwhelming,' says Caroline softly, sitting down with her own cup of tea, 'and if divorce is involved, I'm sure it's extra hard.'

Amanda nods her head vigorously at this statement.

'Everything is hard... and now my husband knows I've left and he's going to come over here and my son is so... so,' she falters, unsure how to describe Jordan, 'so angry and mean.' She feels like a child complaining about a school friend but she is the mother here and Jordan is her son and he should not be scaring her like this.

'Well,' Caroline reaches over and pats her hand, 'I don't know if I have all the answers. But I am here to listen, so if you want to tell me all about it, I'll listen.'

Amanda nods, knowing that she needs to speak to someone, to tell someone. Her mother is gone and her sister is far away and her friends wouldn't understand and some may not believe her but this woman is here and ready to listen and so, before she can stop herself, Amanda begins to speak.

She can feel, as she sips tea and eats too many cookies, that she is spilling out her secrets and that she may regret it but she already regrets so many things she has done. This is just one more thing and all that can go wrong is a neighbour knowing too much about her life. She doesn't mention the text message, the message that she reads every day, sometimes twice a day, the message from someone who wants everything Amanda has and more. She doesn't need to talk about that and she hopes she never will.

She trusts so few people in her life but surely, surely she can trust this sweet older lady.

TWELVE

Caroline

I am devastated for Amanda, for everything she has to suffer through, and I have to admit that now I am even a little afraid for myself. Her husband sounds like the worst kind of man and I know that men like that don't give up easily. He will want her back and he will do what he has to do to make it happen. But would he actually hurt his children? Men do, I know they do. And what will happen if he finds her and turns up here? What should I, as a good neighbour, do? What happens if he turns up and I try to intervene or Gemma does or even Mary? Would he hurt one of us? And if he does turn up and he hurts or kills his wife and children, will we be able to bear the police turning up? Questions will be asked and our lives scrutinised. None of us want that.

And then there is the problem of the boy. It's unlikely that her son will attack her, or is it? She seemed very afraid. Afraid that her husband will find her, afraid that her son is turning into the same kind of man her husband is. He's still so young and he will only get stronger and perhaps angrier.

And what if he decides to take his anger out on me or Mary? He's only a child but we're no longer as strong as we once were. I wanted to know everything but now that I do, I feel like I am somehow involved. I knew she was hiding. The police will protect her from her husband, or so they say, but you only have to turn on the news once a day to know that the police don't always turn up on time, or turn up at all. And even if they manage to make sure her husband never hurts her, she is still tormented by her son.

It is terribly selfish of me to think this but I wish they had never come to destroy our peace. We know who the husband is now and I know how dangerous he is. It would be hideous if he found Amanda, if he came here.

I think about Liam, about how he changed towards the end. He was so nasty, spitting words like 'whore' at me for no reason at all. He would throw things and shout and tell me that I was trying to kill him, and all the time it was going on, I was expected to be kind and compassionate, to nurse him and change his sheets and comfort him when he was sad. Janine never seemed to understand at all but she was living in her own apartment by then, sharing with a couple of friends, and even though I begged her to come home more often she never did. She didn't want to see her father as anything but perfect so I was left to suffer alone with only Liam's nurse for company once a day. She even chose to go on a holiday when he was near the end, which is a callous and terrible thing to do when a parent is dying.

Money would have solved the problem but there was not enough money for full-time care. I was on the waiting list for the hospice when he died. I remember the terrible night before when he had dragged himself out of bed to find me in the kitchen and accused me of cheating on him with the neighbour. I remember laughing, even as tears appeared, because I was so tired. I even laughed as he hit me because I think I was somewhat mad by then.

I realise that I have been standing at the front door since Amanda left, my mind whirling with memories, and I go back to the kitchen so that I can make myself a snack – some crackers and cheese always goes down well. I feed Luna a piece of cheese, which she takes delicately like the lady she is, and then she washes her face and paw. 'You are so polite,' I tell her as she stretches, readying herself for a nap.

Poor Amanda. Bad men can be terribly hard to escape. Mary, Gemma and I know that from experience.

I remember three years ago, being roused by a pounding on the door in the middle of the night. I thought I was being robbed and leapt out of bed, grabbing my gown and the large baseball bat I keep next to my bed.

The pounding continued and I was scared as I pushed my eye against the peephole, only to see Gemma and her little girls in their pyjamas, huddled together on my step, in the cold winter wind. Before that night, Gemma and I had merely been friendly neighbours. She'd moved into the street just after me and I thought her and Rod a lovely couple. He was a nice-looking man, portly and on his way to going bald but he had a pleasant face. Gemma was quiet and shy and came over every now and again to tell me to please let her know if the girls made too much noise in the backyard. I thought that very nice and we had begun having tea of an afternoon now and then. The girls loved Luna and would keep her entertained for some time while Gemma and I talked.

I told her about my life with Liam and how wonderful he had been. He had been sweet, kind and gentle from the moment we'd met down at the local pub. And he was like that our whole married life. Until he got sick.

I remember telling Gemma one afternoon, 'His personality changed. It was quite astonishing. He had been such a quiet and placid man and I know I married him specifically because he was so different to my father. But then he got sick and it felt like many years of rage that he had bottled up inside him came out.'

I never explained what I meant by that, didn't tell her that I believed his awfulness had been hiding for many years, that I understood the vitriol he threw at me in his last year of life came from a deep well of hate he had for me, hate that he had concealed our whole married life. But perhaps she intuited it and felt she could come to me when she was in need.

Of course I let them in that night and I remember my terrible shock at Gemma's bruised face, puffing up as I watched it.

I had never heard a thing, never known what was going on. But then isn't that what they mean when they say that you never know what goes on behind closed doors?

I put the girls to bed in the guest room and it all came out.

'He just gets so annoyed sometimes,' I remember Gemma saying. 'He has a temper and he doesn't mean to.'

I nodded as she spoke, listening while she cried.

'Can't you just... leave him?' I asked her and she shook her head. 'I have nowhere to go, no money, no job, nothing. My mother lives in the US and she always hated him and how would I even get there? He keeps a tight hold of everything. And I wouldn't be allowed to leave the country with the girls. He's a lawyer, and he knows that.'

'There are places that can help,' I told her. 'Refuges,' I said but again she shook her head.

'Those places are not nice and anyway, they're hard to get into. I'll be fine. It just happens every now and again and then he's lovely but he had a bit too much to drink and...'

The conversation went round and around, and in the end, she and the girls stayed in the guest room, all three sharing one bed, and then in the morning, she just went back to him.

I didn't know what to think or what to do because you can't make someone leave a marriage, can you? My mother never did and suffered her whole life. Liam changed at the end of our married life so my situation was different.

I know that I watched a man with flowers arrive at Gemma's house the next day, delivering her husband's apology. I would never have stood for it and I was sorry to know the truth.

And then, only months later, there was an accident.

And quite suddenly, Gemma was free.

Amanda is not free. She is hiding and terrified and she has run away but is still frightened in her own home.

And now Mary, Gemma and I are frightened as well and that really won't do. It won't do at all.

THIRTEEN

Jordan

There is a spot in the park where the Wi-Fi is strongest and I go there with my iPad. I keep messaging him but he just doesn't reply. And now I'm wondering... maybe he won't. Maybe he doesn't want to. Maybe he's had enough of me and Kiera. Maybe he's glad that we're gone.

When I think that, it makes me so mad I wish he was standing right here so I could punch him.

A ball bounces right up to my feet and someone shouts, 'Hey, little help?'

I look at the person shouting and I can see it's someone around my age and I stand up and kick the ball as hard as I can in the opposite direction.

'Arsehole,' I hear as I walk away and I almost wish he would chase after me and try to hit me. Then I could hit him back.

I find another spot in the park and try again, one more time, maybe one last time, and then he can go and screw himself.

Dad??? U have to answer me. U have to!!!

It's getting hotter and I'm thirsty but I forgot to bring some water and I have no money so I guess I'll just have to stay thirsty. I watch the screen, waiting, hoping, waiting some more.

And then a message appears.

Jordan, I'm here. I'm here, mate.

I hear myself make a weird sort of snort noise because I am crying. He's there. He answered me. He's there. I wipe my face quickly and take a deep breath. He doesn't like to see me crying.

dad, you have to come and get me, you have to come. i can't stay here anymore. why haven't you answered my messages? that's why I needed a phone. U have to take me away from here. i told you I should have a phone. all my friends have one and I could have called you. we don't even have a landline at this stupid house and mum won't let me use her phone.

Every second it takes him to respond feels like a million years.

I'm sorry, mate. I was away. You know I was and I didn't check Discord when I got back. But I will come and get you. I don't know where you are. Your mum left without telling me and she's not allowed to do that. She's in big trouble.

I know that's the point. I know Mum doesn't want him to know where we are. I'm not stupid. I lift my fingers to type my reply and then I think about a month ago when I walked into Mum's room when she was changing. I was looking for a charger for my iPad because I couldn't find mine and I thought she was out because it was her time to go to yoga. The door was closed but I thought she was out and I just walked in and she was standing there with only her jeans and a bra on and it was weird to see her and I turned away quickly and said, 'Sorry,' and then we didn't talk about it again.

But I kept thinking about it. I kept thinking about the black and yellow bruise across her stomach, how big it was, how ugly, how it looked like someone had coloured on her skin with a marker.

But I know she makes him crazy. She makes me crazy. She nags us both and she shouldn't do that. And I know that I can't stay here. I just can't.

I want to come home. the address is 24 west street, Delmont. will you come now?

Give me a minute, mate, just let me think.

if you don't come and get me, then i'm just going to come home. i'll walk. i don't care how long it takes.

Jordan, don't be stupid. I'm coming. I'm coming to get you, don't worry. But I don't want her to know. She should never have taken you kids from me. That was a very bad thing to do. And she's going to get into some real trouble. I'll come and get you but don't tell your mum and don't tell Kiera.

mum will worry, but I don't care. i'll leave as soon as i can and message you.

Wait until I'm close, mate. I need to sort some things out at work. And it's better if we do it at night rather than during the day. I'll leave here at around 6 p.m. and it will take me some time to get

through the traffic. Can you get out of the house without her seeing you?

I can. i know how to do it. she won't care anyway. she hates me!!!

She's not a good mother or a good person, but don't worry. I'm coming to get you. I'll message you when I'm close. We're going to sort all of this out, I promise you.

I wait to see if he says anything else but there's nothing. When I look up and around the park, it feels like the sun is much brighter than it was, like there is more light everywhere. He answered my messages and he wants me to be with him.

He will come and get me and I will be at home in my room, in my house with my huge television and my dad.

I will wait at the park as long as I can, even though I'm really thirsty and getting hungry. I don't want her to know what's going to happen. I want her to get a horrible surprise, the same way me and Kiera got a horrible surprise when she told us we were leaving. She deserves that.

I spend the rest of the day gaming until my battery runs out and then I just walk around the park, waiting for time to pass. I don't think about the bruise I saw on her stomach. I don't want to think about that ever again.

All I think about is what it will be like to get out of here. My dad is the best dad in the world and he's going to take me home.

FOURTEEN

Amanda

Her conversation with Caroline feels like it's only made everything worse.

She hasn't been able to stop thinking about it since then, humiliation making her uncomfortable when she thinks about all the details she shared with a perfect stranger. And she has tried to avoid speaking to Caroline, just waving at her if she sees her in the street. Caroline wants to continue the conversation but Amanda can't have that. She knows that Caroline, Gemma and Mary are all friends, that they see each other every day and often spend time together. And she can just imagine what they are talking about. It's a hideous feeling, knowing that you're the subject of gossip. She has a feeling that Gemma would like to come over and speak to her, say hello, be the good neighbour. But so far, the woman hasn't approached her, which Amanda is grateful for. They could be friends in another life, perhaps. But not in this one.

She opens her phone and reads the message again. Maybe

she should just use it, send it to Mike, shock him, unbalance him and get it over with so that he agrees to a divorce?

It could inflame the situation, but how much worse can things get?

She has been in this street for two weeks and it feels like she's aged a hundred years.

Jordan comes home after six and goes straight to his room.

When she calls him for dinner he shouts, 'I'm not hungry,' through the door.

'I'll take him some dinner,' says Kiera when Amanda sighs.

Her daughter fills a plate with spaghetti and a glass with some water and carries it carefully to her brother's room, knocking softly, and then Amanda hears the door open, hears him mutter, 'Thanks.'

At least he's eating. He shouldn't be allowed to lock himself away in his room during dinner but Amanda pushes it to the back of her mind, filing it away with all the other things she will change when school starts, when all this is settled, when she can do anything other than worry.

She and Kiera eat dinner together in front of the television and Amanda is thankful that her daughter is quiet instead of her usual chatty self.

She watches television without actually absorbing what she's watching until after 10 p.m., when she finds she cannot sit still anymore. She is exhausted but wired and she starts pacing up and down the small house, trying to regulate her thoughts. Saying everything out loud has made her fear over what Mike might do worse, so much worse, especially when she saw Caroline's concerned reaction. She regrets talking about Jordan at all because that doesn't feel fair to her son. When this is all over, when she is finally free of Mike and his abuse, she knows she will need to look into therapy for all of them. Can she save Jordan from becoming his father? Surely, it's not too late?

Outside she hears a car in the cul-de-sac and she freezes, standing still in the middle of the living room, straining to listen over her pounding heart.

The car doesn't drive away, instead idling just outside her house, and Amanda thinks she may be sick.

He's here, he's here. Is he? What now?

Forcing herself to move, she goes to the kitchen and grabs her largest carving knife, holding the steel handle tightly, her fingers cramping as she makes her way to the door one step at a time.

She pushes her eye up against the peephole but it's hard to see past the security gate mesh. There's a car there but she cannot see what kind of car. Mike drives a Mercedes like she does but a sedan, not an SUV. His car is black and as she strains to see through the peephole, she can see that the car outside is black as well, the lone streetlight in the cul-de-sac glinting off the metal.

He's here, she's sure he's here. *Oh God, oh God, oh God.* There is a pain across her chest and she tries to take a deep breath but can't.

She grips the knife more tightly and she thinks about getting the kids up and locking them in her bedroom but then what? What should she do first? Where is her phone? She looks around frantically, trying to remember where she left it, and when she can't see it in the living room, she darts to the bedroom, finding it charging next to her bed. With the phone in one hand and the knife in the other, she returns to the front door, pushing her eye against the peephole again, watching the car in the street.

Using her thumb, she taps the zero digit three times and then she waits. The car is still idling. But the moment the door opens and she sees it's him, she's calling the police.

Should I just call them right now?

Yes.

She hits the number, hears it ringing and then a surge of fury runs through her at her own fear, at how cowed she is as she waits for Mike to make a move, and she wrenches open the front door, unlocking the security gate and stepping out into the still warm night air.

And the car, a BMW, drives off, just as she hears, 'You have dialled emergency Triple Zero. Your call is being connected,' and then a man's voice asks her, 'Police, fire or ambulance?'

'Oh, I'm so sorry, I misdialled.' Amanda jumps back inside, her heart racing, the knife still in her hand.

'Is everything okay? Are you okay? Are you safe?' the man on the other end of the line asks her.

'Yes, yes, I'm sorry, I'm so sorry. I just made a mistake.'

'Ma'am, I can send the police out to you right now, all you have to do is say "yes".'

'No, no, I promise you, I'm fine.' She clears her throat. 'It was a misdial, truly.'

'Okay,' says the man but he sounds sceptical.

'Thank you, I'm so sorry to have wasted your time.' She hangs up before the man can ask any more questions. At least she knows they will come quickly, that they will send someone out, but she should have waited.

She is going to go crazy, that's what's going to happen. She is going to go crazy before her divorce comes through. Mike's hold on her is so tight, so complete, that even when they are no longer married, she will still be this strange timid creature.

She returns the knife to the kitchen and grabs a piece of the mint chocolate that she loves, chewing quickly. *It's okay, it wasn't him. Calm down. Just calm down.*

Looking at her phone, she reads over Mike's last text.

Watch out, Amanda. I'm coming for you and I will take away everything you love.

Why hasn't he contacted her since then? What is he planning?

In an effort to distract herself, she goes to the dining room table, grabbing and opening the mail that has been sitting there for days, starting with the information packet sent by the school. She struggles to concentrate as she reads through everything, learning that she should have received a link in her email to fill out all the forms the children need to start school.

Scrolling through her email, she clicks on the link and finds the right forms and begins the laborious process of filling them out. Halfway through she stops. She needs their passports and their immunisation certificates. And she doesn't have them. This thought stuns her. How can she not have them?

The children's passports and their health records are kept in Mike's desk, in a locked drawer. In her rush to get out of the house, she forgot to take these things.

'Shit, shit, shit,' she mutters. She needs this stuff.

If she goes over there, Mike will never let her leave. She could wait, go tomorrow when he will probably be at his store, but then she could be seen by her neighbours, and she may have to answer questions. She's not ready for questions.

And Mike may not be there now. He could be out, she knows that. *You don't know me but...* He could be out.

And if she has the passports and he refuses to grant her a divorce, she could just leave, couldn't she? She could get on a plane to the UK. Paula would send her the money. How could she have forgotten their passports? She doesn't even have her own passport. They're all in the drawer.

A ripple of desperate panic runs through her. They need their passports. You can run if you have a passport. And maybe they will need to run.

She walks over to the children's bedrooms, opening each door with delicate slowness so that she doesn't wake them. She's relieved to see that both of them are fast asleep. Kiera is lying with her arms above her head, her duvet beside her in the warm room and her old plush toy dog clutched in one hand. Jordan is, amazingly, snuggled all the way under his duvet despite the heat. It's unusual for him to go to sleep this early but he must be tired after a full day in the sun at the park, and she knows that his constant anger at her must be physically exhausting as well. She's glad he will finally get a solid night of sleep.

She paces around the house one more time. She surely can't leave them and go check if she can get access to the house. The school will understand, won't they?

But the need for the passports is so strong, it's making it hard to breathe. *I need to be able to run. I have to be able to run.*

Grabbing her keys and hastily scribbling a note for her children – *Ran out of milk, back soon* – she gets into her car.

You shouldn't do this. They are too young to be left alone. Go back inside.

But her hands move on the steering wheel and she reverses the car. He won't be home.

But what if he is? She should just go back into the house and not worry about the documents but what if... Her hands are slippery on the steering wheel. *What if the only way to survive this is to leave the country? I need those passports.*

As fear spreads through her body, she stops the car and gets out, opens the boot and grabs the tyre iron from the spot where it's stored. She puts it on the front seat next to her, feeling safer for having it. Mike is stronger than she is but not stronger than the tyre iron.

Images of Mike sharpening a knife, holding a gun, clenching his fist come to her. He could be preparing to kill her right now. She has no idea if he has access to a gun but he would have access to a knife. Would he use one on her if he found her? The worst time, the most dangerous time, for a woman in an abusive relationship is just after she's left. Amanda has read that many times. She just needs the passports, needs to have them with her and she can't believe she forgot them. *Stupid, stupid, stupid.*

But now is not the time to do this. You've left them alone.

Dismissing the voice inside her head, she speeds through quiet streets, grateful for the lack of traffic which means that a journey of more than an hour only takes forty minutes. She doesn't listen to music as she drives. She needs the silence to concentrate, to get there and then, hopefully, get home.

Jordan and Kiera will be fine for a few hours. They are fine. It's a quiet street, a safe street. They're fine.

FIFTEEN

Caroline

The trouble with getting older is that a full night's sleep grows less likely with each passing year. I have been trying, over the last few weeks, to go to bed later and later in the hope that this will help me get some consistent sleep. I am exhausted by 9 p.m. but if I allow myself to get into bed then and fall asleep, I am up at midnight.

I am watching television at around 10 p.m. when I hear a car in the cul-de-sac and I get up to check who it might be. That's the bonus of living down here, usually only the residents come down here at night, so anything suspicious is easily spotted.

The car idles in front of Amanda's house and for a moment I think it could actually be her husband and I grab my phone, ready to call the police if I notice anything happening. But then, quite shockingly, Amanda's front door opens and she emerges carrying what looks to be a knife. I am unsure what to do but the car drives away and the woman darts back inside.

'How strange,' I mutter to Luna.

All is quiet so I take my shower but when I walk back into my living room to make sure all the windows are locked, headlights sweep across my front window and I am instantly alert. I cross to the window and look out and see Amanda's car leaving.

'What on earth is going on tonight?' I ask Luna, who is following me around, anticipating the small piece of cheese she gets before we both head off to bed, or at least I head off to bed and Luna begins her nightly prowl of the neighbourhood.

I have no idea where Amanda could be going at this hour and I wonder if she has taken the children or if, perhaps, she has a babysitter.

Her house is mostly dark, only the light over the front step left on and a sliver of light coming through the closed living room curtains.

I'm sure she's taken the children or left a babysitter, although where would she have found one in this suburb? She could have asked Gemma, I suppose, but then Gemma would have mentioned it.

Curiosity killed the cat, they say, but I'm not a cat and I can't help myself. 'I'm sure she's not the kind of person to leave her children alone,' I tell Luna as I walk to my kitchen and grab my black torch.

The air is cool as I step outside my front door, the street lit by a single streetlight, the full moon casting shadows and pockets of darkness everywhere.

I listen for the boy's usual shouting at his friends as he games online but for once, since they got here, it's quiet in the cul-de-sac.

Strangled shrieking and the sound of flapping wings fills the air, sending prickles of fear running around my body even as I realise that it's only a large group of fruit bats, hunting for food.

I should go back home where it's safe but I keep walking.

I know that I can go around the side and see into two of the bedrooms, the main bedroom and one of the children's bedrooms. I've visited the house enough to know how to get around the place. I walk slowly, carefully, my feet almost shuffling so that I don't trip.

I hear the purr of a car in the street and I push myself close to the wall at the side of Amanda's house, but the noise fades away just as something runs across my foot and I bite down on my lip, stifling a screech as I shine my torch everywhere, seeking the culprit, but whatever it was is gone. I am far too old to be doing this sort of thing but something compels me to continue.

I make my way slowly to the windows I am looking for. In the main bedroom, the curtains are closed. I try to peer through the tiny gap between them but all is dark.

In the child's bedroom, the little girl's bedroom, the curtains don't quite close, giving me a reasonable view of her bed where I can see her. She is lying with her arms above her head and the covers thrown off and my heart feels like it's being squeezed in my chest. I remember the innocence of childhood. I was a strict mother but children need boundaries.

'Who is babysitting you?' I whisper into the air, shivering as a breeze blows up.

I can't get to the boy's bedroom and I would be fearful of what he would do if he saw me anyway. The house seems dark but he must still be awake. Needing to know if they are being watched, I make my way to the front door and knock quietly, not wanting to disturb the children. But no one answers. I try knocking a few times and then remember that I can see into the living room from the window at the side of the front door. My mouth is dry and I can feel the blood pulsing around my body. If I am caught, it will not look good.

The curtains are closed but, again, they don't quite meet in the middle and I peer inside, expecting to see someone sitting on the sofa but the room is empty and the house is silent.

'Well,' I whisper, somewhat shocked. The children are alone.

I hear a car screeching into the street and I jump, turning and running back across the road. It must be her. When I get to my house, I close myself inside and watch the street through the peephole but the car has gone to a house further up the street.

I cannot believe she's gone out and left the children alone. It's very irresponsible and I would not have imagined that of her.

But now that I know it, I am compelled to do something about it. I suppose I could call the police and alert them. But what would that accomplish? Amanda is suffering and perhaps not thinking straight as she worries over her son and her awful husband. Where has she gone? Perhaps to see him? I hope not as that would be very inconvenient for me. They live far away and that means she will be gone for ages.

'Well, now I'm involved,' I tell Luna crossly and she follows me to the living room.

'Go and find something to do.' I shoo her out of the front door again.

I will have to watch the house until Amanda deigns to return. At least I'm wide awake now with no hope of sleep.

I settle myself down into my chair and grab my knitting, letting the soothing click and clack of the needles comfort me. I am making a blanket for a child. I make them all the time and give them away to church bazaars and the like. This one is blue, or more teal really, Janine's favourite colour.

As I knit, I keep my eye on the house, watching and waiting.

More than an hour passes.

A flash of black across the road startles me and I jump but then Luna turns her yellow eyes to me and I can see by the light of the full moon that she has some creature in her mouth, something small and wriggling with panic.

'Oh, Luna,' I murmur, almost proud of her ability to catch whatever she wants.

I'm sure she will bring it to me when she's done playing with whatever it is.

Janine always wanted a cat when she was little but I never let her get one. Perhaps if I had, she would have been a more pleasant teenager and adult. But perhaps not.

I go over her childhood a lot these days, particularly as we don't speak. I send her messages and she ignores them but I'm sure she reads them.

My hands move quickly and the blanket grows. My knitting efforts are always gratefully received and much is made about how charitable I am. I am charitable and kind, a good neighbour and a good friend to those who need me.

I am a woman who will watch over the neighbour's children when she has gone off somewhere, even though I barely know her. I'm trying to make the world a better place. That's all I'm trying to do.

I peer out of the window again at Amanda's house but all is quiet. And that's just the way I like it.

SIXTEEN

Amanda

As she drives, she takes comfort in the fact that she has Caroline's number because, if need be, she can call her and send her over to check on the children. But she shouldn't have left them and she knows that and still, she can't seem to turn the car around.

Arriving back in the suburb she has fled from is surreal because everything looks so... normal, so familiar, so like her home.

She can't help but compare the wide, tree-lined street to where she lives now and feel some grief over that. She is absolutely certain she will never live on a street this beautiful again. Her children will not have the privileged lives she wanted for them. She is changing everything to save herself and she's not sure if that's fair on them, on Kiera and Jordan who will grow up with divorced parents and everything that comes with that.

As she gets closer to her house, she switches off her car's lights. There is a full moon tonight and she knows her way.

She stops two houses down and climbs out of the car, her

heart drumming in her chest. Before she walks away from the car, she leans in and grabs the tyre iron. It's just for protection. Just in case.

But he won't be home because he will be out, with *her*. That's what she's hoping.

That's a secret she hasn't told anyone, a secret she is keeping to herself in case she needs to use it.

You don't know me but I know who you are and I need to tell you. Mike and I are in love. He told me you won't give him a divorce but I'm begging you, just let him go.

When it had first arrived, she stared at that text for ten minutes, the words swimming in front of her eyes and her heart racing.

It was back in July, the last day of the second school term, and she had been getting ready to go to the end of term concert, slipping her high heels on just before she walked out of the door, when the text came.

And with it, so many questions.

Who is she? Where did Mike meet her? And when? How long has it been going on? And does he hurt her too?

Jealousy burned through her quickly and was almost instantly extinguished.

And then she felt the way she imagined Annette had felt when Mike had asked her for a divorce, when Mike was the one who wanted things to end: relieved.

Because maybe there was someone else to take her place now and so she would be free as well.

It had been so easy to find the woman, to follow Mike one night when both children were at sleepovers, to see where he went. *You can have him. I hope he's what you want*, she thought as she watched her husband embrace another woman. She felt hot tears in her eyes at her echoing of the sentiment from Mike's first wife. Women should listen to each other more. She considered confronting the woman, telling her what she knew about Mike, but then she decided against it, needing only to be free and knowing that the woman was the key to that freedom. Her safety and the safety of her children were more important than anything. So she drove home and waited for him to say something.

But a month passed and then another month, and Mike said nothing and there were no more texts from the woman who wanted her husband. And then Mike talked about Kiera in a way that terrified Amanda and she realised she would have to leave him.

But she has kept the text. She knows who it's from. If he finds her, if he comes to the house she has rented and refuses to grant her a divorce, Amanda will use the text, use what she knows. It's her trump card and the one thing she has told no one about. Not even Paula.

She pulls her phone out of her pocket and finds the message, making sure it's still there, still available for her to use if she needs to. Satisfied that the words have not somehow disappeared, she takes a deep breath, readying herself for what she's going to do.

Taking a look around in case there are any late dog-walkers out for a final stroll, she moves slowly, placing her feet carefully so that she doesn't step on anything that could make a noise.

Feeling like some kind of stalker, she hunches over and makes her way to her house, their house, his house now. His house again. When they got married, twelve years ago, she had been surprised by the fact that Annette, Mike's first wife, had not wanted any part of the house. It was in a beautiful suburb and worth a lot of money and yet Annette had chosen to walk away with almost nothing.

'Why?' Amanda remembers asking Mike when he told her this fact and she also remembers how he sighed and then touched a fingertip to the corner of his eye as though he was trying to prevent tears. 'She just wanted to be free without any responsibility. That's why she didn't want children and why she didn't even want a husband. She only wanted to think about herself and her needs. She wanted to leave the country and she knew I would fight her over the house because I bought it and she hated it but I love it. So, she just left.'

Now Amanda understands why. The loss of the money from the house was a small price to pay for her freedom from Mike. Annette had found someone to take her place, someone who Mike wanted to control more than he wanted to control her. The house was easy to let go of. That's what Amanda has been hoping for from the woman who claimed Mike loves her – an escape route. But it hasn't happened and she has begun to fear it will never happen.

Everything she has ever read about divorce has stated that the number-one rule is not to leave the house, but perhaps that's a rule that applies to couples where the desire to part is mutual and violence is not involved. Amanda has fled with next to nothing in order to get away. Annette did the same thing.

Her feet move slowly over dry leaves and grass and she is grateful that the whole neighbourhood seems to be asleep.

She's still not sure what she's going to do, even when she's standing outside the house, she's not sure of her exact plan.

But then the study lights turn on. It's the only room that she can actually see into from outside the house, a small room that Mike made into his study, where the bookcases filled with books on jewellery design match the timber desk.

The room has a blind but tonight it is open.

She inches closer, her feet almost shuffling so that she doesn't make any noise in the nearly silent street.

And there he is. Her husband, her lover, her friend. Her tormentor. She tightens her grip on the tyre iron.

She watches as he sits down at his desk and picks up a pen,

begins making notes for a moment. And then he drops the pen and runs his hands through his hair as though something has frustrated him. He gets up and takes a book from the bookshelf and opens it, sits down at his desk again, makes some more notes and then draws some pictures. He is looking for new designs, something he does often. He loves that aspect of the business but doesn't have the technical skill to actually make anything.

He looks up and out of the window and she moves sideways quickly, terrified of being seen, her heart galloping in her chest. After counting to twenty, she risks moving to where she can see him again; he is looking down at his book and then he glances towards the bookcase where she knows that one thick black book is actually a lever for the safe room where all the jewellery he brings home is stored. It's a small space with waist-height chests of drawers all around. The children love that room. Kiera loves looking at all the beautiful jewellery and Jordan loves the secrecy of it. She wishes they didn't know about it because she's worried that one day they will go in there and forget that the door locks behind them. No air comes into the room. It's specially sealed to make sure nothing taints the jewellery.

Amanda clenches her fist as she remembers the night Mike locked her in there for an hour, remembers her panic at the idea that no air was coming in, at the idea that he might leave her there until she died. He had dragged her in by her hair after the children were in bed. She'd known it was coming. There had been no shouting and that was worse than the yelling. He had been furious because she'd gone to yoga and hadn't answered his calls even though he'd kept trying to reach her over and again. As she lay stretched out on a yoga mat, she had seen his messages and missed calls pop up on her phone, and she remembers thinking, *Screw you, I'm busy*, even as she had known what it would lead to. She had known that he didn't want or need her for anything important. He had just wanted to know that she would answer, that no matter what she was doing with her day, she would interrupt it for him.

Taking a deep breath, she lets the memory go. *That won't happen ever again. I won't let him hurt me ever again.* It occurs to her as she watches him that she could hurt him. The tyre iron is heavy in her hand. She has the element of surprise and her house key. As she looks at her husband, she wonders how hard she could hit him.

He is wearing a T-shirt and shorts and he looks so... ordinary, just ordinary. He does not look like the monster he is, like a man who would threaten his wife, like a man who would hurt his wife.

And he looks unconcerned. She finds herself angry about this. She is hiding in a rental house, dealing with her furious, aggressive son, and he is just here getting on with his work. He is obviously planning something, obviously pleased with himself over his plans so he can relax. But she is living in terror at what will happen when he finds her. It's not fair, just not fair.

She studies him, studies his bent blond head and notices, for the first time, since he is much taller than she is, that his hair is thinning on top. When did that happen?

Mike is getting old. He is forty-five and while she never imagined he looked his age, she can see a time when he might, can see that time is coming soon.

Again, she is struck by how ordinary he is, how average, and when he sits up and stretches in the chair, revealing his stomach, she experiences a rush of confidence, a rush of energy.

He's just a man, not a monster. He does not have limitless power. He can be stopped. The passports will be hers soon enough.

I don't have to let Mike control the narrative, control my life. I can be the one to take control and I know exactly how I'm going to do that.

Feeling daring, she takes a step closer and then closer again. *You don't get to win. You don't get to be in control.*

Ten minutes later, she is back in her car, her hands shaking, and she releases a giddy laugh of relief. Mike can be stopped, he can be. She starts the car and turns around in the beautiful street, glancing at the time and seeing that she has been away from the children for nearly three hours already.

Panic makes her drive faster and faster, checking behind her all the time in case there are police, but she makes it back to the cul-de-sac in record time, looking around as she parks her car.

Everything is just as she left it, only the cool change of early-morning air is different.

Her hands shake as she gets the key into the lock and then shoves the door to open it.

Please don't wake up. Please don't wake up.

Once she's inside, she checks on the children again. It's nearly 3 a.m. and both of them are just as she left them, and she breathes a deep sigh of relief.

She's too wired to go to sleep so she reads until 4 a.m., when her eyes finally start to close.

As she drifts off to sleep, she allows herself a smile. Mike is just an ordinary man and he can be stopped.

SEVENTEEN

Caroline

I feel my eyes getting heavier as I relax in my chair and I try to remain vigilant but suddenly I jerk awake, aware that I have fallen asleep.

Looking down at my phone I can see that I've been asleep for an hour already and that makes me upset with myself. I was supposed to be keeping watch.

It's nearly 3 a.m. and I look over at Amanda's house just in time to see her car glide back into the driveway. Thank God.

I watch her car, waiting for her to get out. When she finally does, she seems... happy? It's a strange thing to say but she seems lighter in some way. I expect her to go straight into the house but instead she walks around to the passenger side of the car and opens the door, taking something out. There's a full moon tonight so I can see her quite well but I still struggle to see what's in her hand until she moves around to the back of the car, opening the boot. As she leans forward, I see she is holding a tyre iron which she places into the boot, wiping her hands on her pants after she's done. Perhaps she had a flat tyre? I can't imagine she changed a tyre herself. I wonder where she went, if she perhaps went off to meet a new man. Could she be dating already? And so late at night? Surely not. She's not even divorced, and from what she told me, there are many difficult months ahead.

Unless what she told me isn't true. I stand as I mull over that possibility, watching as she goes into her house.

'Well,' I say to myself, 'at least she's home and nothing happened to the children. All's well that ends well.' I know that it's probably none of my business but I do think I will say something to her tomorrow about leaving such young children alone. It is definitely illegal. Anything could happen.

Climbing into bed, I can already feel myself drifting off and I hope that I will, at least, sleep till morning, even as my mind turns over the question of exactly where Amanda has been and why she required a tyre iron.

EIGHTEEN

Amanda

Drenched in sweat, she wakes from a dream where she is looking down at her hands covered in blood, her mouth open in a strangled scream. She's killed someone, someone is dead but she doesn't know who. Her heart is racing as she grabs her phone and sees it's after 10 a.m.

She can hear the television is on and that Kiera is watching something because she can hear Taylor Swift singing. Last night comes back to her in a rush of images and she thanks God that the children are fine, that everything is fine, and she feels like she may just survive this experience now. Mike is just a man, an ordinary man. And she is going to survive this.

Dragging herself out of bed, she goes to the kitchen for a much-needed coffee. Kiera is dancing in front of the television. 'Morning, sweetheart.'

'You slept so late, Mum. Can we go to the shops today? I want to make friendship bracelets to give to new friends. Please, Mum, can we, can we?' On Monday, Kiera will have a week of dance camp, being held at the school she will attend in

February. Amanda is so grateful that the advertisement popped up on her Facebook and that she managed to get Kiera in. It will give her a chance to make new friends, and hopefully some of those girls will be in her class.

Amanda nods. 'We can, just let me eat breakfast and then wake Jordan.'

'Jordan isn't here,' says Kiera and Amanda sighs.

'Where did he go?' Although she knows where he went, to hang out in the park with his iPad, where he won't be bothered by her or his little sister.

'I don't know.' Kiera twirls a piece of her long brown hair. 'When I got up, I saw your note and I went to tell him—'

'You mean to wake him.' Kiera likes company in the morning. She must have assumed Amanda was out and gone to wake her brother to join her for breakfast, something he hates her doing.

'Yeah,' she says, putting the tip of the piece of hair into her mouth.

'Don't do that. Where did Jordan go?'

'I don't know.' She shrugs. 'He was gone when I went to wake him. And then I looked in your bedroom and you were sleeping, just snoring so loud so I didn't wake you.'

'He was already gone?' asks Amanda. Jordan typically sleeps late. But last night he had been asleep earlier than usual so perhaps he has already left for the park.

She goes to his room, knocking softly in case he is actually in there and Kiera has made a mistake. And then she opens the door.

It looks like he's in bed but when she steps closer, she can see that it's just a blanket rolled up under his duvet, a blanket that she stuck up at the top of his cupboard because he won't need it until the weather is much cooler. Why would he have done that?

Amanda swallows as panic ripples through her. She pulls

open the curtains in the room and looks around. Everything is just as it was yesterday when she put some clean laundry on his bed, except the laundry is now lying in a pile on the floor. His backpack and iPad are missing but that's no surprise because he always carries those with him. She searches his room, throwing his duvet off the bed and then getting on her knees to look under the bed even though he obviously isn't there.

'Kiera,' she calls, 'when last did you see Jordan?'

'I don't know,' says Kiera.

Where would he have gone? The park? But it's so early for him. Standing up, she looks around the room where there are still boxes filled with his stuff that he hasn't bothered to unpack. Her gaze falls on his bookcase, where he has unpacked some books and placed some of his special Lego *Star Wars* creations.

Jordan has loved *Star Wars* since he was a little boy and he even sleeps with a soft Chewbacca doll that she bought for him when he was four years old. He would never admit, to anyone, liking the toy next to him as he sleeps. But sometimes when they've had a whole day of arguing, Amanda will creep into his room in the early hours of the morning and stare down at him, sleeping with the doll next to him, and remember that he is still a child.

Turning away from the bookcase, she looks at the bed again. The doll is gone. She does another sweep of the room just in case it's lying somewhere but it's definitely not here.

'Kiera, get dressed, we have to go out,' she calls.

'Yay,' shouts Kiera, who thinks she means the shops but she doesn't.

'No, we have to go and find Jordan,' says Amanda when her daughter comes running into her bedroom.

'But he's probably just at the park. Isn't he at the park?'

'I don't know but we'll go there first.'

Throwing on some clothes and putting her hair up quickly, she and Kiera are in the car in five minutes.

She pulls out of the driveway, her wheels screeching as she makes a quick turn and races to the park.

Getting out of her car, she already has her phone in her hand and she stops people at the park, one after the other. 'Sorry, I'm looking for my son, have you seen this boy, sorry, I'm looking for my son, have you seen this boy, sorry, I'm looking for my son, have you seen this boy?' The more times she is answered with a shake of someone's head, the more intense her panic becomes.

She asks a mother with two young children playing on the swings, a man walking his dog, a group of teenagers all carrying skateboards.

Kiera follows along behind her, occasionally shouting, 'Jordan!'

It doesn't take Amanda long to cover the park. Jordan is obviously not here. Should she call the police? Where else would he be? Where else could he be?

Her heart racing, she herds Kiera back into the car and drives back to the rental house. She can't do this alone, can't possibly find him.

'Go inside, Kiera,' she commands and her daughter obeys her, silent and scared. Amanda follows her in and closes the front door behind them, doing a quick circuit of the house in case Jordan has somehow come home, but he's not anywhere.

'Um, Mum,' says Kiera when she walks back into the living room.

'Yes, baby,' she replies, her mind whirling with places her son could possibly be.

'Maybe Jordan went home.'

'What do you—' she begins to ask and then she stops. He's been very unhappy. It's so far if you're walking but Jordan can be very determined when he really wants something. But surely not...

'No, no, no,' she mutters. Why hadn't she thought of this?

Jordan knows that Mike is back. He went into his room at six last night and said he wasn't hungry at six thirty. He ate the dinner Kiera took him then left the empty plate outside his door, something that irritated her because she hates it when he treats her like she works for him, but she didn't want an argument. It was easier to just pick it up and put it in the dishwasher.

She hasn't heard from him since but she checked on him before she went to try and get the passports. And she saw Mike last night. If Jordan was there, she would have seen him – wouldn't she?

But she had only been looking at Mike, only concerned about Mike. Jordan could have been in the house or on his way to the house. He could have been in his old bedroom, fast asleep.

Why didn't Mike call her to tell her or at least message her? *He wants you to worry.*

She rubs her hands through her hair. She never wanted to have to call Mike. This is exactly what she didn't want. *And exactly what he does want.*

Pulling her phone out of her pocket, she texts her soon-to-be ex-husband, hoping that however angry at her he is, he will at least reply to this.

Is Jordan with you?

Mike, is Jordan with you?

She calls his number, once, twice, three times. He doesn't answer.

What if Jordan is not there? What if he started walking and never made it there?

She puts her hand across her mouth, allows herself a silent scream, her heart pounding. Where is her son?

She calls Mike again, texts him again, calls him again.

And then she takes a deep breath and calls for help.

'You have dialled emergency Triple Zero. Your call is being connected,' the robotic voice tells her and then a woman asks, 'Police, fire or ambulance?'

'My son is missing. He's eleven and he's not here, he's not here.' Her voice turns into a wail on the phone, the surreal horror of her situation making her voice high-pitched with hysteria.

'All right,' says the woman. 'Let's take this one step at a time. How long has he been missing?'

'I don't know,' gasps Amanda as she realises that this is the truth. She doesn't know.

She checked on him before she left and after she came back but she couldn't really see him, just a shape in the bed, so how long has he been gone? *You left them alone and drove off into the night. You are a bad mother, the very worst kind of mother.*

'When last did you see him?'

'Six, six thirty last night.'

'And do you have any idea where he might have gone?'

'I don't know, I thought the park or maybe home,' she replies.

'Are you not at home now?'

'I'm... no, no, I'm not, not at home, I mean,' says Amanda and she bursts into tears because this feels impossible to explain, completely impossible.

Her son is gone.

Is he with his father and safe?

Or is he with his father and in danger?

NINETEEN

Caroline

The screeching sound of Amanda's tyres distracts me from the morning television show I am watching and I stand and go to the window, see her large car roar away. 'I can't abide dangerous driving,' I say to Luna, who I notice has a spot of blood on her whiskers.

'What did you get up to last night, young lady?' I ask her and in response she purrs and rubs herself against me and then sits down to meticulously clean her face.

I am very tired this morning because I only had a few hours' sleep. But I am not one to sleep in so I got up at my usual time but allowed myself two cups of coffee instead of one in an effort to keep myself awake.

I leave the window and go into the kitchen to make myself a cup of tea and return to my show but I've only been sitting there for fifteen minutes or so before Amanda's car comes roaring back.

'She must have forgotten something,' I mutter as I watch her leap from the car and then yell at her daughter to get inside.

But then all is silent so I settle back down again. It's 11 a.m. I will have to take my walk soon because the afternoon will be very hot so I should walk before midday.

Sighing, I get up and go and find my sneakers because exercise is so important for maintaining bone health. Every single post on my Facebook page seems to indicate a different way an older person can hurt themselves and I am drowning in adverts for canes and pills and safety rails.

'Not for me,' I tell Luna, leaning down to scratch her head. 'I am going to be strong forever.'

I grab my phone and open my front door, startled to see a police car cruise into the cul-de-sac. I hastily step back and return to the living room, peering out through my net curtains as I watch two constables get out, a man and a woman. They walk towards the house, both of them putting on their hats and the man tucking in his shirt before he rings the bell.

'Oh my,' I say to Luna. Grabbing my phone, my walk forgotten, I call Gemma.

'The police are in the cul-de-sac,' I tell her when she answers. 'Something is going on at Amanda's house, I thought you would want to know.'

'Okay... okay,' she replies and then, rather rudely, she hangs up.

I call Mary next and she doesn't even say hello. 'I've seen them,' is how she answers.

'Do you think this is about the husband?' I ask.

'Well,' says Mary slowly, 'it's not like we're strangers to the police turning up, are we?'

'True,' I say as I remember the terrible morning that the police came to tell Gemma about Rod, about how he had been found, lying on the side of the road, his head bleeding.

He was in his running clothes because he had gone out the night before for his usual evening run.

No one had seen what had happened but he was found in

the early hours of the next day by a passing motorist. The night before, and later than I like to be disturbed, Gemma had come over to tell me she was worried about him.

'He left at seven and he's usually back by eight but it's nearly nine thirty,' she said. 'Should I go out and look for him?'

I can still recall looking at Gemma, who was wearing a long-sleeve top despite it being a rather warm night in summer, and knowing that she was concealing terrible bruises.

By then I had been encouraging Gemma to find a way to leave but whenever she seemed determined to go, Rod would lure her back with words of love and gifts. I found it very frustrating.

'He'll turn up,' I told her. 'Perhaps he's just met a friend for a drink?'

It was a strange conversation, both of us saying all the right things, even as our faces reflected something entirely different.

I saw the police arrive in the cul-de-sac the next morning. I didn't even wait to be asked for my help because I knew she would need help.

I hurried over to her house and knocked on the door, only to be told the dreadful news that Rod was gone. Gemma was shaking and crying and the little girls were shocked into silence. The police asked me if I knew anything else but I explained exactly what had happened the night before, even remembering the time Gemma had come over because it did bother me that it was so late.

And then I took the girls away with me so that Gemma could have some time to get herself together then go and identify him, a concept so awful that I can't quite imagine what it must be like.

She told me the police believed it had been a hit-and-run and that there had been no witnesses at all. There is a stretch of road just before the highway that Rod used to like to run along, and for some reason it has very few street lights and no cameras anywhere. After the accident, I did write to the council, expressing the need for more lights and a camera but when Rod was hit, there was nothing. The council ignored me, as they usually do.

'Indeed, we do know,' I tell Mary now. 'And just like I helped Gemma, I will go over and see if Amanda needs help as well.'

'No, don't do that. Give the woman some space and some time. We don't know exactly what's happened and we don't know her very well.'

'Well,' I say, 'we have some idea.'

'Caroline, don't go over just yet. I'll go into my garden and see what I can find out. I'll let you know when you're needed.' I knew Mary would say this. Gemma and I don't always tell Mary everything we are thinking and feeling. She's old and some of her behaviours are quite concerning, like her belief that her son is living overseas with his wife and children, but she is always useful if you need some information. No one thinks older women are a threat.

I let a sigh of frustration escape my lips because I really want to help Amanda but I agree to wait.

Mary calls back twenty minutes later.

'Well, my goodness, that didn't take very long,' she says excitedly.

'Tell me.'

'Almost as soon as I got out there the little girl, Kiera, came out into the garden and spotted me and waved.'

'Okay...' I often find myself frustrated with the way Mary tells a story but she has information and I want it so it wouldn't do to upset her by hurrying her along.

'She told me her brother is lost and the poor little thing

looked so sad, I wished I could reach over the fence and give her a hug.'

'Oh dear,' I reply because sometimes it's better to simply murmur along in a conversation with Mary.

'I thought she would tell me more but she starting doing cartwheels on the lawn – do you remember being able to do a cartwheel, Caroline?'

'I do.'

'We were so young once but we knew so very little. I remember when I turned cartwheels on the lawn, when I moved my body with grace and lightness. I am so far away from those days that it's hard to believe that once I was able to make my body do whatever I wanted it to. Once your knees have been shattered, you are never the same again.' Her voice catches slightly as, no doubt, terrible memories return.

'Oh, Mary,' I murmur because it's not often that she admits the truth of what happened to her but I need to keep her on track. 'Did she say anything more?'

'Well, I said that her mum must be very worried about her brother and she said... give me a moment... she said, "I think she's kind of glad he's not here."'

'What a strange thing to say.'

'Yes, and when I asked her how long he had been lost for, she told me that they didn't know because he wasn't in his bed this morning.'

'Poor Amanda.'

'Indeed, and when I asked her where she thought her brother might be she came right up to the fence and whispered that she thought he had gone home. Her mother came out then and called her in, so that's all I know.'

'Well, thank you, Mary, at least we know what's going on now.'

'Yes, but the police are here, Caroline. I hate it when the police come, you know that.'

'They will only want to talk to you, Mary,' I soothe her. 'And the boy could be found soon enough and then this will all be over.'

'I know, Caroline, of course I know that.'

'Have a cup of tea,' I suggest, 'and a bit of a rest. If the police come to your house, give me a call and perhaps they will let me sit with you.'

'Thank you, Caroline. I don't think they will allow that, but thank you.'

I know she's right. They will want to interview us separately, to gain as many perspectives as possible.

Once I am off my phone, I find myself needing to do something. I decide on pickling the few kilos of baby beetroot that I have set aside for this. It's heavy work to do during the day when the air is so warm but I need to keep myself occupied. I am somewhat oversupplied with pickled vegetables this year but I do so enjoy the process, and it will give me some time to think about what is going on at Amanda's and how I can best help her.

It's what I do, after all. Help.

But first I need to get some empty jars from the basement, where I store them.

I keep the door bolted closed because on more than one occasion I have woken to the sound of shattering glass in the middle of the night only to find Luna on one of the shelves, mischievously pushing jars off with her paw. It's a great deal to clean up so she needs to stay away from the basement.

I unbolt the door and walk down the stairs into the room where it's lovely and cool. Humming softly, I pick up some empty jars, looking forward to an undisturbed hour or two of using my hands.

TWENTY

Amanda

'Go and play in your room,' Amanda tells Kiera when the doorbell chimes but Kiera will not move and Amanda doesn't have the energy to force her to do anything. But when she opens the door and Kiera sees police uniforms, she immediately bolts out into the back garden. Amanda wants to go after her, to comfort her and calm her down, but knows it's for the best, even if she can't shield her from all of it. Amanda briefly considers taking her over to Caroline's but she doesn't want to involve her neighbour in her drama until she has to. *Please let me not have to tell anyone, let them find him and bring him home.*

At the front door are a man and a woman in their uniforms.

'My name is Constable Simpson and this is Constable Stern,' says the woman, her black hair tied back in a short ponytail.

'Come in,' says Amanda, stepping back and letting them in, conscious that the living room is very warm. She goes to open more windows, glancing out at the garden where she can see

Kiera talking to the old woman who lives next door. 'Kiera,' she calls, not wanting the child to say anything to the neighbour. Kiera moves over to the fence and seems to whisper something to Mary before spinning around and coming back inside.

Amanda's heart is still pounding with panic but she feels better now that the police are here. They will find Jordan soon. They have to.

'I was just talking, Mum, I was telling Mary about Jordan being lost,' says Kiera. Amanda feels frustration ripple through her body. Obviously Kiera was sharing the news and Amanda can sense that soon the other women who live in the cul-de-sac will know what's happened and she can already feel their judgement seeping through the thin walls of the small house. Good mothers don't lose their children.

'Go to your room or stay with me, but stay out of the garden for now,' she tells her daughter, trying to keep her voice moderated so she sounds calm even though she would like to snap at her chatty child. She turns to face the police officers.

'Can I get you some tea?' she asks. 'Or a drink, or...'

'No, we're fine, thank you,' says Constable Stern. He has brown eyes and a brown beard and offers her a quick smile.

'You've reported your son missing. Why don't you start at the beginning.'

Amanda sits down on a chair and the constables take the sofa. Kiera climbs onto her lap, which irritates Amanda, but she puts her arms around her daughter, feeling her warm skin, holding her tight. 'Give me a few minutes to talk to the police, okay?' she says to her daughter. 'You can go and look at my make-up,' she adds, knowing that Kiera loves to be able to look through her things. Kiera obediently gets off her lap and leaves the room.

It takes ten minutes for her to explain, including that she saw Jordan last night and that she popped out for milk but forgot her purse so came back and then just got back into bed because she was tired and then when she woke up, Jordan was gone.

It's a convoluted story and she comforted herself, as she prepared it, that her lies are only white lies because there's no way she's telling the constables that she left the children alone in the middle of the night to drive to her former home.

'Okay,' says Constable Stern, writing everything down in his notebook, 'so you think he might have tried walking home to see his father?'

'Yes. He's been very unhappy about the move, like really angry, and my husband got back nearly a week ago from a trip to China—'

'Just to be clear,' interrupts Constable Stern, 'when last did you actually speak to your son?'

Amanda drops her head. *You're a bad mother, a terrible mother. What kind of a mother doesn't know if her son has left the house? What kind of a mother leaves her children alone at night to go and get something she could have done without?* Her behaviour last night was irrational; getting the passports had felt imperative, but this morning, she finds herself unable to justify it.

'At six thirty, I called him for dinner and he said he wasn't hungry but Kiera took him a plate and I know he ate it because it was outside his door at around seven, I think. And then at around ten last night, I checked in on him and he was sleeping so I didn't...' She stops speaking. Jordan is never asleep by ten, never. He stays awake far later than he should, gaming online.

Last night she was so troubled, so worried about Mike turning up and then so panicked at the idea of not having their passports, that she didn't even think about the fact that her son seemed to be asleep at 10 p.m. Why didn't she click that something was off, wrong? She's been so self-absorbed, so concerned with how she is going to get through this.

'Oh God,' she gasps, 'I thought he was in his room at ten... I checked but maybe I was wrong. I don't know how long he's been gone.' Amanda sits forward in the chair and buries her head in her hands, breathing deeply so that she does not cry. She needs to answer their questions. If she can hold it together until she's answered their questions, they will find Jordan. It's magical thinking but it's all she's got.

'And has he taken anything with him?' asks Constable Stern, and Amanda sits up again, clenching her fists and pushing her nails into her palms.

'He has his backpack but I'm not sure if he has taken extra clothes in that, because it looks like only one set of clothes is missing, maybe two, I don't know. He has his iPad.'

'Right, and does that have a location app?' asks Constable Stern.

Amanda shakes her head. 'I disabled them all, everything. I didn't want... want my husband to know where we are.' Her breath catches in her throat. *How could you have been so stupid?*

The constable nods and even though he is looking at Amanda with compassion, Amanda can feel herself being judged.

'Can I have a recent photo of him?' asks Constable Simpson, and Amanda hands the woman her phone, her screen already open to the last picture she took of Jordan. It was at his end of year school concert and he is wearing a wide smile, joyful at the prospect of the long summer holidays. Amanda feels a heavy guilt as she looks at the picture. She knew what she was planning to do only a few weeks later. And it's all gone so horribly wrong. Is Jordan with Mike? Did he make it safely there?

'Right, I've sent that out and I've told everyone in cars to be on the lookout. We have a couple of people back at the station looking into the routes he could have taken, but if we don't find him soon, we will go to the press and circulate a few pictures of him.'

'And will someone go to my house, I mean the house where I used to live? Maybe his... my ex just doesn't want to tell me he has him. I'm sure he's there.' She can hear the hope in her own voice. It means Jordan is safe, even if he's run away to be with his father, even if this now makes things more complicated, at least he's safe.

'We have already dispatched a team to go there so we should know soon if he's there or not,' says Constable Stern and then there is nothing to do but wait.

'Should I go out and look for him?' she asks but the constable holds up a hand to immediately stop her.

'Let's check where we can right now and if we haven't found him in an hour, we'll call in the State Emergency Services to begin searching the neighbourhood.'

Amanda can't sit still. 'I may just get a drink,' she tells the constables, who don't even hear her because they are both on their phones.

She doesn't go to the kitchen, but rather to her bedroom, where Kiera has obviously grown bored with looking through her make-up and gone back to her own room. She goes into the en suite, where she closes the door and turns on the basin taps, the rushing water loud in the small space. And then she gives in to her tears, covering her mouth so Kiera doesn't hear her.

She slides down onto the floor, remembering a fight with Mike in a hotel room. They had hired a babysitter to stay the night with the children. Jordan was seven and Kiera was five and they were supposed to be celebrating their eighth wedding anniversary.

She had been excited for the night away, eager for a long bath and a lovely dinner without having to worry about being interrupted.

It had been a perfect evening. She had enjoyed her bath with a glass of champagne, and before they had gone out to dinner, Mike had given her another beautiful piece to add to her collection of jewellery: a large sapphire surrounded with diamonds sat in her ear with a thin white gold chain dropping to another smaller sapphire. The earrings were beautiful – a little too heavy to wear but Amanda knew better than to say anything.

'They're amazing,' she told him. Dinner was perfect and when they got back to their hotel, the sex was, as always, wonderful.

'We should do this more often,' Mike said, 'it's so nice to have you all to myself.'

She laughed. 'I know, but those little darlings are going to be with us for many years so we have to just work around them. And it is nice to be alone but I have to admit that I miss them, don't you?'

'Not really,' he said. They were lying in bed together, their fingers interlaced.

'Well,' she said, 'unfortunately you can't put children in a cupboard,' and then she laughed because it was a joke, just a silly joke.

'But we could look into boarding school.'

Shocked at the idea, Amanda let go of his hand, sitting up and pulling the sheet to cover herself. 'I would never do that. They're so little, and even when they're older I don't believe in boarding school.'

'Well,' he said, 'what you think isn't really that important.' The words were said slowly and she knew by then to be on the lookout for when Mike began to speak slowly. It meant that a whole lot of other things were going through his mind. It meant that despite his measured tone, he was working his way up to something. But she'd had a lot of wine with dinner and champagne before dinner and she wasn't as alert to the signs as she should have been.

'They're my children,' she snapped, 'and you won't tell me what to do with them.'

He moved so fast she didn't even understand what he was doing. In a second, he was next to her, his hands buried in her hair, her neck snapping back as he pulled. Pain seared through her body as she gasped for air. He put his face right next to hers as his other hand grabbed at the skin on her back and pinched hard. 'Don't,' he whispered in her ear, 'ever talk to me like that again.' He released the skin on her back and slapped her, hard, so she pitched forward on the bed, some of her hair coming out where he was still holding it.

He let go and stood up. 'I can end your life in a second, Amanda,' he said, 'and those are my children and I will decide what happens to them.' And then he got off the bed and went into the bathroom, leaving her shocked into silence.

And yet she still slept next to him that night, curled up small in the bed, waking frequently when he moved in case he was going to hurt her again. Why did she let it go on for so long? *Now is not the time to think about that.*

Mike is furious at her for leaving. And he thinks the children are his property, just things that belong to him that he can discard or change at will.

She bites down on her lip, trying not to think about what he might do to Jordan, what exactly Mike might be capable of. She is holding her phone in her hand so she texts him again.

> *Please, just let me know if you have him. I'll come home if you just reply and we can just pretend this never happened.*

As she sends the text, she feels a part of her dying inside. The small defiant, hopeful part that wanted a life free of fear and violence but she is willing for that part to die to make sure her children are safe.

But her phone remains stubbornly silent.

Mike wants her to suffer, to worry, to panic.

As she listens to the rushing water in the basin, she wonders how much Mike wants to hurt her. How much does he want her to suffer, and what might he do to his son to make sure that Amanda knows exactly how angry he is?

What exactly is her husband capable of?

TWENTY-ONE

Caroline

I wait for more than an hour, watching Amanda's house, not moving from my chair. I need to know what's happening.

My phone rings and I see it's Gemma. 'What's happening?'

'Nothing as yet, the police haven't come out again. Mary says she went out into her garden and Kiera was also outside. She told her Jordan is missing. I'll let you know when I know more.' As I finish that sentence another car pulls up, but this time, the car is not marked as a police car. When two people get out of it, I understand that my little street may be in more trouble than I thought. I wish this woman had never come to live here with her horrible son and her secrets but now that she is here, I have to try and help her. It's my duty as a neighbour. The two men who have climbed out of the unmarked police car look to be detectives, their badges on lanyards around their necks. I knew they would be here soon. This is how things go in this situation and I knew they would be here.

I call Mary. 'Detectives have arrived and I'm sure they will come and talk to all of us. I will come when they are at your house but if they won't let me stay you need to be careful what you say to them.' Mary has some idea of how things have unfolded but she doesn't know everything. There is a lot that Gemma and I have just kept between us.

'I'm not stupid, Caroline, and I know what to say to police.'

'Yes,' I agree because I can feel when Mary is ramping herself up for an argument. 'But maybe...'

'Maybe what, Caroline?' she asks and I have a flash of memory of Mary ten years ago on the day I moved in. I was busy directing the moving men on where to put everything when she came across the road. She was so much stronger then, walking well and standing tall despite her constant knee pain and her limp, her dyed brown hair tied back in a neat bun.

'Welcome,' she said when she saw me, handing me a blue and white patterned plate with a lovely sponge cake on it.

'Thank you,' I replied, taking the plate, 'I'm so happy to be here.'

I invited her in and we chatted about this and that, things like what day bin collection was and Liam's death. I knew we would be friends forever, knew that we would be able to share our secrets with each other. And, of course, we do know each other's secrets. So many secrets.

'Maybe don't mention James,' I say, biting down on my lip as I say it.

'Hmph,' says Mary and I know that I've made her angry because a fantasy is easy to hold on to if no one ever challenges you on it, easy to stay locked inside of because reality causes too much pain.

'Promise me you won't talk about him,' I say now because I need her to promise.

'If I do, they'll just dismiss me as a mad old lady.' I can hear I've upset her.

'Well, mad old ladies rarely get into trouble.'

'Yes,' she agrees. 'I have to go, Caroline, and don't worry. I won't mention my boy.' She hangs up and I sit back in my chair, a jittery feeling inside me, like an itch I can't get to. I want this to be over, to be done, but I have to let it play out.

Mary doesn't want to talk about James, about how he died and how long ago he died. She doesn't want to talk about the arguments the boy had with his father, the screaming, vicious arguments. Or about any of the other things Dan, her husband, did. But then no one in this little cul-de-sac wants to discuss those they've lost. It's all too sad and perhaps my life would be easier if I could live in the fantasy as Mary does and believe that Liam was still alive and still like his old self. But I can't because I know the truth. So here I am in the present, trying to make the world safer in my own way. And some days it's very tiring and I'm not sure I'm succeeding.

The detectives have arrived at Amanda's house and that means that things are getting more serious.

And I know that none of us will ever be the same again.

TWENTY-TWO

Amanda

It feels like nothing is happening, like no one is out looking for her son, and Amanda cannot sit still. Kiera is sitting at the dining room table now, colouring in, her usually chatty child silent with the seriousness of it all. The two constables are on their phones, making and receiving calls every two minutes it seems.

'We have people looking,' Constable Stern keeps reassuring her but Amanda can't bear the wait.

'Are you sure that I can't go out and look for him, maybe ask some of the neighbours to help?' says Amanda to Constable Simpson when she has finished her call.

'As I told you, Mrs Caldwell, we have people looking and we will be calling in the State Emergency Services once we have ascertained that he is not at your former home.'

'But I can't just... sit here.'

'If you could give me a moment,' says Constable Simpson as her phone begins to ring again.

Amanda stalks away, furious at being dismissed. Each time

Amanda goes up to one of the constables with another idea of what might have happened to Jordan, she is told that they are 'exploring all avenues'. It's maddening.

She goes into the kitchen, where she fills the kettle to make herself another cup of coffee. She's had two cups already and she really should stop but she needs the jolt of energy caffeine gives her. She has offered the constables coffee but both have declined and now she wants to shout at them to tell them to just go out and look for her son. Mentally, she keeps going through the route she drove back to her house last night, trying to imagine where Jordan could be and if there is anything dangerous along the way. But it's mostly double lane roads, some with pavements on the side, some without. If Jordan had been hit by a car, would they know? If he was lost, would he know to go and ask for help? And if he asked for help, would he find the right kind of help? The world is filled with terrible people, Amanda knows that, but she also knows that sometimes, the most dangerous people are those you live with, those who are supposed to love and care for you.

Hunting in the cupboard for some chocolate to go with her coffee, she hears the front door opening and nearly drops her cup as she places it in the sink because obviously, he's back, he's home and all this was for nothing. She darts out of the kitchen but it's not Jordan standing in the small living room but two men in suits with lanyards around their necks.

'These are Detective Sergeant Sanders and Detective Senior Sergeant Chen,' says Constable Stern, 'and they just need to have a chat with you about this situation.' Amanda stares at the detectives, unsure what to say.

'Kiera, why don't we go for a walk outside?' says Constable Simpson. 'You can show me where the park is that Jordan likes to go to.'

'Mum?' asks Kiera, and Amanda feels cold in the warm room, as though winter has suddenly descended in her house.

'It's fine, baby,' she says and Kiera hops off her chair and goes to grab her sandals. Her daughter wants to be away from here, out of here, and Amanda doesn't blame her.

Once she and the constable have left the house, Detective Chen indicates the sofa. 'May I?' he asks and Amanda nods, sitting on a chair opposite him, his dark eyes intently focused on her face. *Just tell me, just tell me please, just tell me what's happened.*

'Mrs Caldwell, we have a record of you calling Delmont police station about your husband about a week ago.'

Amanda nods.

'We've listened to the call,' he says as the other detective, Detective Sanders, who has a bald head and a potbelly, walks around the living room looking at family pictures of Amanda and the children, only of her and the children. She didn't need any of Mike around the place. Amanda nods, unsure where the detective is going with this.

'On the call you stated that your husband had threatened you for leaving him?'

'Yes, he told me I would regret it. I can show you the text message.'

'Yes, that would be good.'

Amanda pulls her phone out of her pocket and finds the messages, handing it to the detective.

She watches him scroll through, watches his eyes move over the words, and she folds her arms across her chest. She is dressed in a soft blouse and linen pants but she feels naked, exposed.

'Right,' says the detective, handing the phone back to her.

'He wasn't happy about me leaving him.'

'And when last did you see your husband?' the detective asks.

Amanda bites down on her lip because there's no way she's going to confess to last night, no way she's going to tell this detective she left her two underage children alone at night to go and get the passports she left behind. It was a moment of madness, she knows that, and mad mothers have their children removed.

They will take Kiera from her. Can they do that? She's sure they can do that.

'He was in China when we left. I haven't seen him since the day he left,' she says, making sure to uncross her arms and to look directly at the detective, actually at a spot just between his eyes so that she keeps looking at him, despite wanting to look away.

'Right.' The detective turns to look at his colleague, who is now standing next to him.

'Mrs Caldwell, police have been to the house, to your former home to see if your son is there and—'

'Oh no,' moans Amanda because here it is, here it comes. If they had found him there, they would just say. If they had found him there and he was fine, they would just say it but not if he wasn't fine, not if he was hurt or... She rocks forward and puts her head on her knees, suddenly dizzy. And then she sits up and clenches her fists. 'Did you find him? Did you find Jordan?'

'No, Mrs Caldwell,' says the detective.

'Then why,' she takes a deep breath in and out, 'then why aren't the SES here? Why aren't we all out looking?'

'Because, Mrs Caldwell,' says the detective with an infuriating emphasis on the word *Mrs*. One day she will change her surname and not be connected to Mike, one day.

'Because?' she asks.

'Because when we tried to locate your husband to ask about your son, his store manager told us that he hadn't come into work. And when our constables got to the house, they could not get hold of your husband. He didn't answer the door despite his car being in the driveway. They conducted a walkaround of the property and found the back door unlocked. They accessed the property and discovered your husband in his study.'

'Okay,' says Amanda, not sure what the detective is getting at.

'And he's dead, Mrs Caldwell. We believe the cause was blunt force trauma.'

The detective sits back and takes out a small notebook as sirens ring in Amanda's head.

'I don't...' She can't even push a sentence out because she doesn't understand. *Dead. Mike is dead?*

'Now, Mrs Caldwell,' says the detective, and Amanda feels her stomach churn, 'on the basis that we will be checking traffic cameras from here to your former home over the last few days, I want to ask you once again. When did you last see your husband?'

TWENTY-THREE

Caroline

When the doorbell rings, I am busy carrying Luna up the stairs from my basement storage space.

I had been expecting the police much earlier but hours seem to have passed so I stopped waiting for them and got on with my day. But now my heart races at the thought that they are here, at the idea that they may have many questions to ask and not just about the missing boy.

I wanted to go outside, to stand on my step and look over at Amanda's house and hopefully see a policeman or woman come out so I could ask some questions myself but I have resisted. The less I am involved now, the better.

But finally, it seems they are here.

To my surprise, standing at the door is not the police but a volunteer from the State Emergency Services, or the SES as they are known. I recognise the orange vest. Looking past her, I can see that in the time I have been in the kitchen and then down in the basement, the street has filled up with people all wearing orange vests. Two more police cars have arrived as well.

I should have been watching. But it's all happened very quickly so obviously the search is now being ramped up.

'Hi, my name's Michelle.' She has a squeaky voice that instantly grates. She's very young and looks positively excited to be standing on my doorstep. Her hair is in two plaits which is a style that belongs on children.

'Hello,' I reply cautiously.

'Yeah, um, so you may have seen that the police are in the street and it's because we're looking for the little boy that lives in that house.' She turns, pointing to Amanda's house. 'He's gone missing and we wondered if you had seen him. I have a picture here.' She takes a picture out of her pocket. In it the boy is smiling, not an expression I've seen on his face once since he got here.

'How long has he been missing?' I ask.

'Well, um, we're not really sure but do you remember the last time you saw him?'

'Well,' I say, casting my mind back to yesterday when everything was different and when I still had some hope that we would have tranquillity in our street again. 'He went to the park yesterday but I did see him getting home at around 6 p.m.' This is the truth because I was out front watering my thirsty rose bushes then and I remember seeing him arrive home, his back slouched and a scowl on his face. He saw me but didn't even bother with a slight nod of his head, but I didn't expect friendliness from him. I would have settled for politeness but he didn't offer that either.

'Okay, yeah, so we know he came home last night but his mother hasn't seen him this morning. You didn't happen to see him this morning, did you?'

'No,' I say, 'but I was doing some pickling this morning. I was making pickled beetroot and so I was very busy.' I show her my hands that are, somewhat alarmingly, stained with red beet juice. I should have worn gloves but part of the enjoyment of the pickling process is being able to touch and smell the vegetables. I don't like the feel of those gloves or their plasticky smell.

'Right, um,' she turns to look behind her and I can see the volunteers all in a group, one of the constables talking to them, 'could we just have a look through your house and garden, to see if he's here?'

I laugh at her, unable to help myself. 'My dear girl, I live alone with my cat. I think I would have noticed a child in my house or garden. Perhaps he has run away to be with his father; you know that they're separated and I don't believe it's very amicable. He wasn't very happy to be here,' I tell her as she nods, listening intently.

'Right, um, okay, thanks. If you wanted to help, we're going to be going through the whole neighbourhood, and we could really use as many boots on the ground as we can get.'

'Certainly,' I tell her because I'm capable of walking around the neighbourhood and doing my best to help. And I ought to participate in the search. It's what any good neighbour would do. 'I'll get some shoes on and come out and join you all in a few minutes.'

'Okay, thanks,' she says, her desire to walk through my house forgotten. I certainly was not going to let some stranger wander through my space tracking in dirt and germs. Ridiculous that she thought I would.

I watch as she walks over to Gemma's house to, no doubt, say exactly the same thing. I keep watching while Gemma opens her door and steps outside to listen to the young woman.

Gemma looks up at me and I give her a wave, which she doesn't return. We don't like the police and all these people here in the street. It feels like we're being invaded and, not for the first time, I wish that Amanda had never chosen our cul-de-sac as the place to run away from her marriage. I feel sorry for her, naturally, but Mary, Gemma and I have earned our peace and now this woman has destroyed it.

I go back inside to get a proper pair of sneakers.

Making sure my house is locked securely since there are so many strangers milling about, I make my way over to the group of volunteers, where I am joined by Gemma.

'Where do you think he could have gone?' I ask Gemma when we are standing with the group, watching as a few people turn towards us to hear Gemma answer the question.

Gemma shrugs. 'I thought he would have gone home.'

'We know that Jordan is not at his former home,' says the constable, handing out neighbourhood maps.

'How do you know that?' I ask and he sighs, irritated at my question. 'He may be hiding somewhere or just lost.' Someone hands me a map and I take it although I don't actually need it.

'We can walk together,' says Gemma and I nod.

We have a lot to discuss, a lot to talk about, and its best we do that far away from everyone when we do.

TWENTY-FOUR

Amanda

It's after 2 p.m. and Amanda cannot begin to think how to process her thoughts, how to work out what to say to the detectives who come back to her every fifteen minutes or so to ask if she remembers anything else about last night. They have obviously decided she hurt Mike, despite knowing that Mike was the one who abused her. She can see it in their faces, hear it in the way they phrase their questions as they hope to catch her out. Do they know something? Inside her, fear and worry fight for space as she tries to concentrate so that her answers remain the same.

How long until the police find her car on the traffic cameras? Does it take days or weeks? Should she tell them? They suspect her, clearly they suspect her. She is grateful she thought to put the tyre iron back where it belongs when she got home last night. Imagine if they asked to look through her car...

And to make things so very much worse, her feelings about this are tangled up together: her love for Mike, her hate for

Mike, her fear of Mike. But he is dead, dead. How can he be gone? After everything she has been through, everything she has been worrying about, he's just gone?

Blunt force trauma, a blow to the head. With what?

'We don't know,' Detective Chen said when she asked, 'but we will know soon. Is there anything you would like to say about last night, anything at all? And I must caution you that we will find out if you have been near your former home.' It's a phrase he keeps repeating as he looks straight at her, and she can hear that he is trying to get her to tell him the truth, that he knows he just needs to keep asking and eventually she will give him the answer they want.

Will they arrest her when they find out? Who will care for Kiera? She can't go to prison. She needs to find her son and get out of here, go away and be somewhere else.

How can Mike be dead? He has loomed so large in her life for the last fourteen years that it seems impossible, and for a moment she wonders if he's not dead, if this is all just a ploy by the police to get her to confess to leaving the children alone, but surely they don't do that. They're not allowed to do that, are they?

'Where did you find him?' Amanda had asked.

'He was in his study, lying on the floor by the bookcase.'

'His study,' she repeated, dropping her head into her hands, seeing him there last night, just last night.

The front door is open and she has a view of the cul-de-sac outside. She has seen Caroline and Gemma go off to look for her son, has watched others, all strangers in orange vests, set out to find him as well, and she has watched as the groups of twos and threes trickle back into her front yard, all shaking their heads as they see the constables and then getting new routes to walk. Each time a pair or a group of people return, her heart sinks because she knows it means they have failed. There are police looking all over the city, along every conceivable route back to their home, and yet no one has found anything. Jordan could be anywhere, but so far, Jordan is nowhere.

Mike is dead and someone killed him.

Detective Chen has been outside but now he walks back into the living room and sits down on the sofa opposite her.

'Where's Kiera?' asks Amanda because she hasn't seen her daughter for at least an hour. Should she tell her about her father? Could she tell her? No, not now, not with her brother missing. There will be time for this terrible news later, when Jordan is home, when what's left of her family is together. And that's a sad truth that keeps punching her in the gut. Mike was her family. She knew they couldn't stay married and she was afraid of him but she also still had the moments of happiness in their marriage stored inside her, like the days their children were born, holidays as a family, moments of watching him teach Jordan and Kiera to ride their bikes, Christmas mornings. If it was all just terrible, it would have been so much easier to leave, but it is never all just terrible, never just that.

'She's in her room with Constable Simpson, but we did want to ask if you thought there was somewhere she could spend the night. I realise this is a very difficult time but perhaps it would be better if Kiera was being cared for.'

Amanda opens her mouth to tell the detective that she can't let anyone know where they are, that she is essentially hiding, but then she realises again and her eyes fill with tears. Mike is gone and is no longer a threat. *Isn't that what you wanted? Isn't that the best-case scenario? I thought it would be but now that it's real, now that I'm here, I don't know. Mike is dead and no longer a threat but the children have lost their father, the father they adored.*

'Mrs Caldwell,' says Detective Chen, dragging her back into the small living room where people are standing around, looking at her things, taking up space. Judging her. Definitely judging her. She can feel it in the air.

'I can call someone.' She picks up her phone from the coffee table and calls the mother of Kiera's best friend, Nellie.

'Amanda,' says Sasha when she answers the phone, 'I've just seen the Amber Alert on the news and I went to the house but it's all cordoned off by police tape. What on earth has happened there? Have they found Jordan?'

Amanda stifles a scream because she would like to scream and she can't have this conversation now. 'Sasha, I need your help. I'm going to give you an address, it's far away but I need you to come and get Kiera and,' her voice shudders, 'just keep her for a couple of nights, please.'

'I don't understand, where are you? No one has heard from you for a couple of weeks. You didn't return my calls and I wanted to get the girls together.'

'Sasha, please, I... I just can't explain right now. But I really need some help,' Amanda says, her voice cracking as she wipes away stray tears.

And Sasha obviously registers this. Sasha is a patent lawyer and very capable as well as being a wonderful single mother to her daughter whom she chose to have alone.

'Give me the address. We'll be there as soon as we can.'

Amanda recites the address and hangs up with relief. 'I'll just go and get her ready,' she says to the detective, who nods.

Kiera is regaling Constable Simpson with a story about her Barbie doll who looks to be on holiday in her camper. 'And then, Ken sings a song but Barbie has no time for that and...'

'Kiera, honey, Sasha is coming to get you and you're going for a sleepover at Nellie's house. Isn't that nice?'

The constable stands up and leaves the room.

'But I'm not allowed to tell Nellie that we're here, it's a secret. How will she know where to find me?'

Amanda breathes slowly in and out. 'I called her mum and

she's coming to get you. It's okay for Nellie and her mum to know.' *Now. It's okay for them to know now.*

'Where's Jordan?' her daughter asks, and Amanda can hear the suspicion in her voice. Children pick up on everything.

'We're still not sure, sweetheart.'

And at that, Amanda slumps down onto the bed, exhausted, devastated. Kiera stands up and comes over to her, leaning her head down on her mother's shoulder. 'He'll come home, won't he, Mum? He's a bit mean but he's my brother and I want him to come home.'

Amanda wraps her arms around her daughter and holds on tight. 'He will come home, I promise,' she says, even as she realises that she should not be making this promise. She has no idea where her son is, where he could have gone. He could be anywhere at all. Lying on the side of a road, taken by someone who offered him a lift, anything could have happened and she feels a shiver run through her body.

She lets go of Kiera and rubs her cheeks, getting rid of any evidence of tears. 'Now let's pack up your stuff. You go and stay with Nellie and have lots of fun and then when you come home, you and me and Jordan will get the biggest pizza ever.'

This will not be home for much longer because Mike is gone. But will she be able to return to the house where her children have lived their whole lives or will she be going to prison? Will she return there with two children or with one? The questions circulate in her mind, jabbing at her so she feels the physical hurt of these terrible possibilities as a sharp stabbing pain in her head.

'With pepperoni?' asks Kiera.

'Yes, and ice cream for dessert with chocolate sauce and sprinkles.' When this is over, the promise of a treat will never be the same for her children or for her. When will this be over?

'Yay,' says Kiera and Amanda stands up because she can't sit still while she is lying to her daughter. She gathers the things Kiera needs, filling her purple backpack.

Holding Kiera's hand, she walks into the living room where there are three police officers and two people wearing orange vests. Kiera steps closer to her, shy in front of all the strangers.

'I'll take her outside to wait,' says Constable Simpson, and Kiera gives her mother a hug and then willingly takes the constable's hand. The constable is a young woman and she probably doesn't have children yet but she's very pretty and Amanda imagines that she has someone at home, someone she will go home to and talk to about her day, about a missing child and a murder. Amanda would like to be the one to leave, to go home, to be anywhere but here, anyone but herself.

She returns to her chair in the living room just as Caroline walks in through the open front door and comes over to her. 'I'm so sorry, Amanda. I'm sure we'll find him.'

Amanda feels irritation at the platitude rising inside her. But what else can Caroline say?

'Thank you,' she replies, hoping that will be enough for Caroline.

She is filled with regret at sharing anything with the neighbour because she knows that Caroline is judging her, everyone is.

The only person she really wants to talk to is her sister and she's not going to call her until she knows something concrete about Jordan. Paula is too far away to do anything except worry and it's not fair on her. And how on earth will she tell her about Mike, how will she explain it all?

'Have you eaten anything?' asks Caroline and Amanda shakes her head.

'I'm not hungry.'

'Nonsense, there are people outside handing out snacks to the volunteers but I think you need something more substantial. I'm going to go home and make you something.'

'Please, you don't have to do that.'

'Nonsense. We're neighbours, and in this street, we help each other.'

Amanda feels tears appearing again and she swipes at her face, nodding.

'This will all work out for the best.' Caroline leans down and pats her hand. Amanda has no idea what to say to that. Caroline doesn't know Mike is dead because the police don't want to announce it yet, not while they are still looking for Jordan. 'The two may or may not be connected,' Detective Chen has said.

Caroline leaves and Detective Chen sits down opposite her again. Amanda would like to get up and go hide in her bathroom and scream but she knows she can't.

'We've looked all through your family home a couple of times,' says the detective, 'and there's no sign that Jordan was there. You husband is a jeweller so we are looking at the possible motive being robbery. I assume that there's a safe somewhere, but our officers haven't been able to find one.'

'It's not a safe,' says Amanda, 'it's a room and it's behind the bookcase in the study.'

'Right, and do you know how we get in?'

Amanda looks up at the detective as she thinks about the specially built room, thinks about the hour she spent locked in there and her panic over running out of air. If Mike goes into the room, he always leaves the bookcase door slightly open. It's a good place to hide if you don't have to be there for too long. *A good place to hide. Jordan knows about the room.*

'There's no air in there.' Panic ripples through her. 'If he put Jordan there, there's no air in there, there's no air!' she shouts.

'I don't think... How do we open it?' asks Detective Chen, something like panic appearing on his face for the first time since he got here.

For a second, everything she knows flies out of her head as all she can hear is the rushing white noise of dread.

'Mrs Caldwell,' snaps Detective Chen.

'There's a black book without anything else on the spine, a big black book, you just pull it and the door opens. It just swings open.'

Detective Chen leaps up, his phone at his ear.

TWENTY-FIVE

Caroline

Gemma and I walked around the neighbourhood following groups of others, eventually peeling off by ourselves. I talked and Gemma listened. She's good like that.

'Let's go back,' I say to her eventually. 'There are enough people looking and I want to see how Amanda is doing.'

When we get back to her house, I have to push past an annoying number of people. It's dreadful to have so many nosey parkers in our little cul-de-sac, all of them studying us, all of them filled with questions.

In the house, Amanda is hunched over in a grey armchair, her gaze focused on the front door but her mind obviously somewhere else. The poor thing looks so thin, so frail, as though overnight she has shrunk and she's only known about her son missing for a few hours. A whole day hasn't even passed yet. I feel very sorry for her pain. I am sure that this will all be sorted out by tomorrow but I can't say that to her. There are no guarantees in this situation.

After I've spoken to her, offering the only help I am able to right now, which is to prepare some food for her, Gemma and I return to my house to make Amanda something to eat.

'I can do chicken sandwiches,' I say as I open my fridge. 'Do you think she would like that?'

'I have no idea.' Gemma slumps into a chair. She wore inappropriate footwear for our walk and now her feet are in pain.

'We have to help in some way,' I tell her.

'You mean we have to be seen to help,' scoffs Gemma.

'You're very casual about all of this,' I say. 'Imagine if one of your girls was missing.'

Gemma flicks her white-blonde hair over her shoulder and shrugs. 'But they're not, are they, Caroline? And they never will be. My girls are safely at camp and when they're here, they're well behaved and kind to everyone. I know that Amanda loves her son but he's not a nice kid and we don't actually want him back here. Whatever has happened is probably for the best,' she says although she has the grace to blush when she says this and then her eyes shine slightly with unshed tears and I know that she's very upset for Amanda.

'Yes, well,' I say to her as I slice some sourdough bread and cut up fresh roast chicken, adding pickled cucumbers and other vegetables, 'we wanted her to leave, didn't we?'

'Yes,' agrees Gemma. 'But this is... all these police. I hate it.' She sniffs. This is something she has said more than once already as we walked and I grit my teeth, annoyed at her repeating what I already know. I have a feeling that there is something Gemma is not telling me, something she is not saying, and I do so hate it when people keep secrets from me.

'It's just unfortunate about the boy taking off and running away,' I say instead of anything else.

'I thought you were watching the house. It's strange that you didn't see him. Are you telling me that you didn't see him at all?' Her tone has changed to one of belligerence, as though this is my fault.

'No, I didn't see him at all or I would have said something to the police. And as far as we know, the boy could have left any time after six. I assumed that she left both children alone in the house but perhaps she knew he was missing last night. Perhaps that's where she went, to look for him.'

'Then why didn't she tell the police that?'

'I have no idea,' I say with a shrug.

'You're absolutely sure you didn't see him in his bed when you went around the house to check?'

'I told you, Gemma, I couldn't see into his window. Anyway, what difference does it make now?' I slice the sandwiches into neat triangles, always the nicest way to eat a sandwich. 'The boy is missing and needs to be found.'

'And you have a plan to help,' says Gemma, somewhat sarcastically. She really is getting on my last nerve today.

'Right now, I am making sandwiches, that's what I can do to help right now.'

'Maybe Amanda really didn't need your help, Caroline. Maybe we should all have just accepted that they would be here for six months and left it at that. We could have survived six months.'

I step away from my sandwich, my knife still in my hand, and I go over to Gemma, leaning in close to her in case anyone is somehow listening. 'We all wanted our peace back, Gemma, and it's not my fault the child ran off.'

Gemma stands up and moves away from me. I know that I can be quite scary sometimes but I'm not in the mood for her nonsense today.

'You owe me, Gemma.' I gesture at her with the tip of the knife, which is rude of me but I am making a point. 'Don't ever forget that.'

'How could I, Caroline?' Her fake blue eyes fill with the tears that have threatened to fall all day but I don't succumb to overly emotional behaviour.

I smile, and then chuckle. 'Goodness, Gemma, stop being so dramatic. I'm going to take this sandwich over to Amanda and then pop in on Mary. I'm sure she's dying for an update on the search.'

'I'm going to... I'm going home.'

'I'll call you tonight and then we can talk, sort through things.' She needs to know to be home to answer my call. 'It will be late, so don't go to sleep,' I add.

Gemma nods without saying anything else and leaves. Honestly, since her husband died, the woman is positively skittish sometimes. I suppose an early death makes everyone think of their own mortality. Liam was only fifty-nine when he was diagnosed with lung cancer and it spread so quickly to his brain. I did try to get him to give up the smoking. I nagged him for our whole married life, pleaded with him, begged him really to take better care of himself but he never did. And then when he got sick and became so awful to live with, everyone expected me to carry on and just accept it. And how was that fair? Janine didn't want to be involved. She just wanted me to be there, day and night, accepting Liam's awful abuse while she got on with her life.

It was a relief when he died and I'm not afraid to acknowledge that. And if that child never returns home to torment his mother and grow up to be like his father, that won't be the worst thing and I'm not afraid to acknowledge that either.

I tut as I cover the sandwich in tinfoil to take over to Amanda. What she needs is something to eat, something to keep her strength up.

As I'm leaving, I lock my front door behind me, noting that there are fewer people in the street now. People get tired and soon they will be sent home for the day. I wonder when they will find the child, if they will find him at all.

People disappear all the time and Australia is a big country with lots of places for people to disappear to.

As I cross the street, I watch as two constables climb into a car and speed off, tyres screeching, and then I see a detective come out of the house, talking fast and jabbing the air with his finger.

Something has happened. I walk closer to the house and hear Amanda wail from inside. 'No,' the word stretching and filling the air.

Something terrible has happened. Still clutching my plate, I turn and go home.

This is not the time to deliver sandwiches, not the time for me to be there.

I will wait until I know more. Only then will I know what I have to do.

TWENTY-SIX

Amanda

'No,' Amanda wails, 'no, no, no, no,' she repeats. This cannot be possible. It simply can't be possible.

But quite suddenly, it seems to be the only logical explanation. Hideous images of her child gasping for air appear in her head and she wants to be sick.

Would Mike have hidden Jordan in there or would Jordan have gone in himself? Both children know how to open the door. It was a fun secret in the house but they have also always understood that this was Daddy's work and they are not allowed in, but if Jordan wanted to hide, he may have chanced it.

Maybe Mike was killed in a robbery while Jordan was in the room, hiding away. Maybe Mike had no idea Jordan was even in the room? Is that possible? Or did Mike put Jordan in there, did he put him in there for a reason?

Why haven't they opened the door, why don't they know the answer already?

It seems that hours have passed but she knows it's only minutes, only a few devastating minutes.

'Okay, okay,' says Detective Chen, coming back to the sofa, holding up his hands as if to stop Amanda's escalating panic.

'We've opened it and he's not in there.'

'Oh, thank God, thank God.' Her stomach is churning, her mouth dry. *He's not in there, not locked inside gasping for air or dead. He's not in there.*

But he's still out there somewhere, alone and maybe hurt. She closes her eyes, tries to think of the right prayer to say so that her son returns to her.

'Mrs Caldwell,' says the detective and Amanda looks at him.

'He was there.'

'What?'

'He was there. They found his backpack, the one you said is missing. It was in there. It was there, but Jordan wasn't.'

Amanda stares at the detective, sure that this must be some sort of joke. Her mind throws up a thousand possibilities as the detective watches her.

'If he was in the house,' she says, wrapping her arms around herself, holding her fear for her son close and tight, 'and he heard something or saw what happened to Mike...'

'Perhaps but...'

'If he saw something and then ran away, he would be trying to get home, to get back to me. I know he would.' She closes her eyes and sees her son, running through the darkness, terrified and lost. He's still her little boy, will always be her little boy. Does he know about his father? Did he hear it happen? Did he see it happen?

'I need... a moment.' She stands and leaves the room for the safety of the bathroom where she can lock the door.

She sinks to the floor, too numb to cry, too dazed by what has happened to form coherent thoughts. Instead, she just sits, staring at the green tiled bathroom wall, Jordan's favourite song from when he was in preschool going around in her head. *The wheels on the bus go round and round...*

She holds her phone in her hand, watching the minutes of this terrible day pass one after the other, the song going around. *The windows on the bus go...*

After twenty minutes there is a soft knock on the door but she ignores it. Ten minutes later there is another knock and she knows she cannot hide in here forever so she stands and leaves the bathroom, returning to the living room where the detectives are waiting with their questions. At some point, as the song played in her head, she made a decision. She will tell the truth now.

She has no choice.

'Mrs Caldwell,' says Detective Chen, his irritation at having to wait for her obvious in his strained tone, 'our constables at the house have looked through the drawers and they can't tell if anything is missing but we are assuming that if it was a robbery, everything would have been taken.'

Amanda nods her head as she sits down in the chair she feels she has been sitting in forever. They are right. If it was a robbery, everything would have been taken. The jewellery stored in those drawers is worth hundreds of thousands of dollars. Just before she left, she went into the room and looked through those drawers, wondering how much she could take. How quickly would Mike notice if a piece was missing, and would he think to check? In the end, she had left it all, along with the furniture, taking only the pieces he had gifted her. *You can have it all if you just let me leave.*

'So, at this point,' says Detective Chen, 'we are again looking at this being targeted and personal. I have to ask you again, Mrs Caldwell, did you go anywhere near your former home last night?'

Amanda opens her mouth to tell them everything because

maybe, if she throws herself into the fire by admitting she left her children alone, that will be what's needed to save her son.

She is stopped from speaking by a knock at the front door. Detective Chen stands and opens it. 'Thanks,' Amanda hears him say and she looks up to see him holding Jordan's backpack.

She stands and moves towards him, holding out her hand for the black backpack with a picture of Mario from the video game *Super Mario Bros.* on the front. The detective hands it over and she clasps it close to her, holding it, hugging it in the way that she cannot hold or hug her son. *How has this happened? How is it possible? Mike is dead and Jordan is missing? How am I standing here right now in the middle of this nightmare?*

'His iPad is in there and we're hoping that you know how to unlock it,' says the detective as Amanda moves back to the chair, frustrated that she cannot go to her bedroom and go through the backpack alone, without being watched by the detectives.

She opens the backpack, her hand touching his soft Chewbacca toy first. She pulls it out, feeling her heart contract. It will be dark soon and he will not have a place to sleep, not have his comfort object, even though he would deny that it is. Placing the doll to her side she pulls out a couple of pairs of underwear and some socks along with two T-shirts and a pair of shorts. Perhaps he only meant to be with Mike for a couple of days or perhaps he thought that Mike would get him what he needed.

Her hands touch the iPad in its black case and she pulls it out, dropping the backpack to the floor and touching the screen, which lights up. The battery is at twenty per cent.

'What we're hoping to find is a message he may have sent to someone, maybe a friend, anything that can tell us what he was thinking and where he might be.' Detective Chen sits down on the sofa opposite her.

Amanda keys in the code to open the iPad, which is Jordan's birthday. She's glad that he hasn't changed it, that he has not pushed against her rule that she be able to open his iPad. It was a rule made when the children were first given the devices but she has never thought to check on what they were doing. Kiera comes to show her everything she is looking at and Jordan is forever in the middle of a game. Perhaps she would know more about her son, would be more able to connect with him, if she was aware of exactly what he was doing online.

'Could he have been communicating with his father through this?' asks the detective as he laces his fingers together, and Amanda can see from the way he is sitting that he would like to grab the iPad and conduct a search himself.

'No,' says Amanda, 'no, he can't... He talks to his friends through Discord, but he...' She stops speaking. 'Shit,' she whispers softly.

'Mrs Caldwell,' says Detective Chen.

'Discord, the server. Mike joined to keep an eye on Jordan while he was gaming. He could have been speaking to him through that. I didn't, I just didn't...' She shakes her head as her hands move across the screen and she finds the server, opening it up. The detective comes to stand behind her, peering over her shoulder as she finds the right place. And there are the messages between Mike and Jordan.

'Oh God,' says Amanda as she scrolls through, 'he was talking to him. Mike came to get him, he just...' She covers her mouth with her hand as she comes to the last few messages.

please dad please let me out. please i'm sorry if I made you angry. please.

dad, are you there??? please let me out i can't breathe in here please.

dad? can I come out now can you get me out?

dad, you need to open the door and let me out. mum said we should never be in here with the door closed because there's no air in here.

will you let me out please??? i'm starting to feel weird can't you hear me shouting, please?

please dad, please please let me out. why won't you let me out. are you mad??? i'm sorry, please just let me out. my throat is getting sore.

dad, stop shouting at mum, please stop screaming. just let me out and i'll go home with her. i can't hear what you're saying but please just let me out now i can't breathe dad i can't breathe.

why won't you open the door??? just open the door mum is right, u r an arsehole i hate you. JUST OPEN THE DOOR!!!

i'm sorry dad i didn't mean that please just open the door.

dad!!!!!!!!!! please, i can't shout anymore. dad, I

'You were there,' states the detective, his voice clipped and precise.

Amanda feels her eyes fill with tears. 'I was there.'

TWENTY-SEVEN

Caroline

My doorbell rings as I sit down in front of the plate of pesto pasta I have made for myself. I have no appetite but I need to eat because it's important to keep my strength up.

I shake my head as I stand. Surely the volunteers should have been sent home by now. Perhaps because it stays light for so long, they will be out much later, but how much more of this neighbourhood do they need to cover?

It's not someone from the SES but rather two constables. 'Caroline Morgan?' one of them says, a woman with short brown hair.

'Yes?'

'We just wanted to ask you a few questions, if that's okay.'

'Questions about what?' I reply, little shocks of fear flickering through my body.

'May we come in?' the other constable, an older woman with hair cut like mine, asks.

'You may.' I step back and then turn, leading them into my living room, where the younger woman sits down next to Luna on the sofa and strokes her, forcing Luna to leave her comfortable spot. Luna does not enjoy being handled by strangers.

'We just wanted to ask a few questions about the Caldwell family.'

'Of course.' I have been waiting for them all day, and now that they are here, I remind myself to remain calm and composed. It's difficult but I have dealt with the police before. 'I assumed you would be here much earlier.'

'Well,' says the young woman, 'the situation has evolved in the last few hours.'

'How so?'

She gives me a small smile. 'Nothing that we are at liberty to discuss, but we did want to ask you if you noticed anything about the family, anything that concerned you.'

'Well...' I wonder exactly how much I should tell them. 'The boy was quite volatile. I know that he was unhappy to be here and I have to say that I'm not surprised he ran away. He hated it here and told her so, quite loudly and often.'

'Did you see him yesterday?'

I tell the women exactly what I told the SES volunteer, that I saw him return home at 6 p.m. and then not after that.

'And did you hear any arguing or shouting last night?' She is making notes on her phone, which I find quite disconcerting.

'No, it was quiet for once. I suppose I should have found that strange because he usually games late into the night and disturbs Mary, she can tell you that.'

'Mary lives next door?' the older constable asks, looking through her notebook.

I nod.

'So, you didn't see anything unusual last night?' the younger constable asks again, and again I shake my head. 'He came home at 6 p.m. and I heard nothing after that. I went to bed at 11 p.m. as usual.'

I am not going to tell them I watched Amanda leave, that I

saw how long she was gone and that I watched her return. Those are Amanda's secrets and I will keep them as I keep all my neighbours' secrets.

'Now if there are no more questions,' I say, standing up.

'Just one more,' says the older woman. 'Do you think Mrs Caldwell is capable of hurting her children or... anyone?'

A brutal question that I have no idea how to respond to.

'She's been here two weeks,' I tell them. 'I don't know her well enough to make that assumption but if you ask me, her husband was more than capable of such a thing.'

'But you said you don't know her that well. Did she speak to you about her husband?'

'Only a little.' I flush, irritated at myself for allowing them to lead me here. I have no idea how much they know, how much Amanda has told them.

'What exactly did she say?' asks the young constable.

'Just that... just that she was separated and her husband was... not very nice.'

'She said that?' asks the older woman. 'That he was not very nice? Did she say anything else?'

I feel like one of those people in horror movies that the audience always screams at to 'get out now' but I cannot get myself out of this so easily.

'She told me she was afraid of him. That's all she said. That's why she was here, because she wanted to be far away from him.'

The young constable nods her head. 'And you didn't see her leave the house last night, did you?'

'I... no, I didn't. I was watching television. I don't make it a habit to watch my neighbours,' I lie. This is getting very complicated and I can only hope that when they speak to Mary and Gemma, they get exactly the same story. They should. We have discussed it enough.

'Okay and—' begins the older constable but I have had quite enough of their intrusive questions.

'If you will excuse me,' I say, squinting my eyes slightly, 'I have a terrible headache. Walking around in the heat was a bit hard for me today.' I try to appear older and frailer than I am.

I don't wait for them to respond, simply walk to my front door with my heart hammering in my chest. I rub the side of my head dramatically.

'Do you need to see a doctor?' asks the young constable, all kindness and concern now.

'I need to lie down,' I tell her.

'We may need to return with some more questions,' says the older woman and I nod my head as I show them out.

'I'll be here,' I assure them even though the urge to pack up my car and leave is almost overwhelming. They are going to look into me, I know that.

And this boy needs to be located before they can find out anything about me.

TWENTY-EIGHT

Amanda

'I was there,' she repeats.

She has no idea how to play this, or if it even matters anymore. If they take her children away because she left them alone, does that matter if they are safe? If she loses them but Jordan is safe, will that make up for it? Will they take them away? Will there even be two children to take away? She shakes her head and then buries her face in her hands, pressing against her eyes until black spots appear.

'Mrs Caldwell,' says the detective, 'I need you to tell me the truth now.'

Amanda sits up and leans back in the chair. 'I needed the passports,' she confesses. 'I left them behind and I was filling out school forms and I just needed them and I couldn't believe I had left them.' She explains what time she left, how long she was gone and what she was doing there. 'But I didn't go in the house. I swear I didn't go in the house,' she says, shaking her head as she wraps her arms around herself.

She remembers thinking that Mike was 'just a man' because

that's what he was, just an ordinary man, and how much relief it had given her. She had looked up at the full moon, taking a deep breath in and letting it slowly out, releasing her fear. 'I'm going to be fine,' she whispered. 'We're going to be fine.' And then she slowly crept away from the house, back to her car, reminding herself over and again that soon she would be free of him and she didn't need to confront him. All she needed to do was wait.

Was Jordan in the safe room when she was outside staring at Mike? If she had gone in, could she have saved her son and brought him home?

'So you're saying that the woman that Jordan is talking about in the messages to his father, the voice he heard arguing with your husband while he was locked in the safe room – that was not you?'

'It wasn't,' says Amanda. 'I promise you it wasn't. I... I was scared of Mike, just so scared, but I needed to get the passports. Then I got there and... I don't know. I watched him for a few minutes, and I felt better and calmer, because I realised he was just a man...'

'Who could be killed?' asks Detective Chen softly.

'No, no, no,' says Amanda vehemently. 'I wouldn't have, I didn't. The children loved him. I wouldn't take him away from the children.'

'You understand that I am not sure I can believe you.' And now the other detective, Detective Sanders, comes to sit down on the sofa as well. He has been mostly outside, mostly organising the searchers.

'I didn't kill my husband.' She feels a bubble of hysteria rising inside her. This is absurd. She covers her mouth with her hand, biting down on the flesh of a finger so she can regain some control. Taking a deep breath, she looks directly at the detectives. 'I didn't kill him. I didn't go inside the house at all. I watched him through the window and then I came home again.'

'Your son would recognise your voice, wouldn't he?'

Amanda shakes her head. 'It's hard to hear in the safe room.'

'But his message states that it was you.'

'And I'm telling you that it wasn't.' She shakes her head again.

The detective studies her for a long time, as though his dark eyes could somehow penetrate into her mind and discover the truth.

'Are you going to take Kiera away from me?' she whispers because she needs to know.

'That will be a matter for social services, but right now your daughter is safe and we have to find out what happened to your husband and where your son is,' says Detective Chen.

'Mrs Caldwell,' says Detective Sanders, his mouth turned down, 'I want to ask you a difficult question.'

Amanda clenches her fists – how many more difficult questions can there be?

'Do you think your son is capable of hurting anyone?'

'What?' Amanda throws her hands up. 'He's eleven. That's ridiculous.'

'I understand. But your son is quite tall and you have explained that there were... tensions in the marriage and... that you and Jordan have been fighting...'

'Just stop.' Amanda knows what the detective is trying to say. 'My son would not have hurt his father. He adored him and even though he knew that Mike and I fought, he didn't... didn't know about the rest of it.'

'Sometimes children know more than we think,' says the detective softly.

'So that's it?' she asks, her voice rising. 'That's all you've got? Either I killed Mike or his eleven-year-old son did? That's what you've come up with?'

'Mrs Caldwell, we are only trying to understand what has happened here. You have lied to us about where you were last night and now your husband is dead and your son missing. And while we are not sure until we see some sort of inventory list, none of the jewellery seems to have been taken so that rules out robbery as a motive.'

'I can't... I just... I need to rest.' She gets up. 'Unless you're going to arrest me,' she spits, furious at everyone and everything.

'Not tonight,' says Detective Chen ominously.

Amanda folds her arms and turns away, going into her bedroom and throwing herself down onto her bed. Could Jordan have hit Mike, hurt Mike? Does Jordan know about Mike hitting her? He loves his father very much but might he want to protect her if he did know?

Terrible images of Jordan hitting Mike, of Mike hitting her, of Mike lying on the floor and Jordan being locked in the safe room swirl around inside her. Her eyes are burning and she closes them for a moment, sinking instantly into sleep.

Some time later she opens her eyes with a jolt, sitting up and immediately dashing to the living room, her mouth dry and her heart racing.

'Ah, Mrs Caldwell, we were just leaving. We will be back early tomorrow morning. You should get some sleep.' Detective Chen is standing by the front door, his notebook in his hand.

Amanda glances down at her phone in her hand, sees that it's nearly 9 p.m. 'So no one is looking for my son. He's out there, alone and lost, and you're all just going home?' Her voice catches in her throat and tears appear.

'I can assure you that we will have the night patrols searching for him, but right now it's best we all get some rest.'

'Then I'll go and look for him.'

'Please don't leave the house for any reason. He may return home and then you need to call us immediately,' instructs Detective Chen.

Amanda nods, because she knows this is true. She wouldn't

want to be out if he came home. She needs to be here, to keep watch. *Come home, Jordan, please come home. Come back to me.*

'And we would prefer that you remain here while we investigate what has happened to your husband.'

Amanda opens her mouth to say 'ex' but then she doesn't say anything.

Detective Chen studies her. 'There will be a car stationed outside if you need anything at all.'

They suspect her of murder. They are watching her, even if they have said the car is here in case *she* needs anything. She suddenly feels very trapped in this small house but she is unable to protest.

They are not arresting her but they are, in fact, making sure she doesn't go anywhere. She is being watched. *Do I need a lawyer? Where do I get a lawyer? Do I call my divorce lawyer?*

'I'll be back in the morning.' Detective Chen nods his head and Amanda does the same, too defeated to have an argument. She cannot believe that this is where she finds herself, alone in some far-away suburb. She thought she had planned this well, that she had covered all the angles, that getting a lawyer and moving out was the right way to go. But now she is here. *You'll regret this, I promise you'll regret this.*

Mike's words assault her as surely as if he was standing here in front of her. But she will never see him again and the children will grow up without a father.

Once everyone has left and the house is quiet, she texts Sasha, asking about Kiera.

> *The girls are having a lovely time. Please don't worry. Just try to get some rest. I hope he's home soon xx.*

She goes into the kitchen and begins washing cups that have been used for tea, and wiping down the counters. She thinks about making herself some dinner. She is hungry but she can't contemplate eating. What if Jordan is hungry?

Jordan was in the house, in their home, in the safe room. How long was he there and why would he have been in there? Did Mike know he was in there? *He's not there now.*

Sighing, she fills the kettle, determined to have a cup of herbal tea instead of yet another coffee.

The house is so quiet now that everyone has left, the silence an eerie reminder that she is completely alone. She supposes that she could call Caroline and ask her to come over but she doesn't know the woman very well. It's late anyway.

In her pocket her phone buzzes, and she pulls it out, seeing a text message from an unknown number. *Maybe it's him. Maybe he's asked someone to borrow a phone.*

A flame of hope flickers inside her as she opens the message.

She reads the text quickly, her heart sinking as she instantly realises it's not about Jordan, but then she reads it again, more slowly this time.

You should check out this article about your neighbour.

There is a link to the article and Amanda's thumb hovers over it for a moment. There is an Amber Alert out for her son and the world is filled with lunatics. Is this some kind of scam?

What's the worst that could happen? The worst has already happened.

She clicks on the link, and it takes her to an article from 2012. Using her finger and thumb she blows up the grainy black headline.

WIFE ACQUITTED OF HUSBAND'S MURDER

TWENTY-NINE

Caroline

I am sitting in my living room in the dark, watching Amanda's house, waiting to see her light go off. I watched everyone leave, saw the constables and the detectives go. But I can also see that a police car is still here, taking up space in our cul-de-sac, watching us all. That's a problem. Not an insurmountable one, but a problem I need to consider.

It's 10 p.m. and far too early for me to go to sleep but Amanda really should go to sleep because she needs her rest. I'm sure tomorrow will be another difficult day for her but I do hope they find her son safe and sound. If they don't, I wonder if she will stay here in this neighbourhood, if she will remain in the house until the owners tear it down. I am sure the police have been to her former home. They must have been. I would have liked to ask her about that. Her husband hasn't turned up here to help look for his son of course. Men like that are only interested in themselves.

I can see that Gemma is still awake and that Mary has gone

off to sleep. She was jittery when I spoke to her after the police had been over to her house.

'They asked so many questions and I'm sure I got some of the answers wrong.'

'They are concerned that Amanda may have hurt the child,' I explained, 'that's all.'

'I told them about the shouting. I told them he pushed me.'

'It's fine, Mary. I'm sure it's all fine.'

'But what if they come back? What if they know about James and Dan?'

I do feel so sorry for Mary. She's had a difficult life. She worked as a nurse for many years, tending to everyone with kindness, and yet at home, she was tormented by her husband, by his violence that was eventually turned on her son. I have known her for many years and I have always known about her son, about what happened to him, exactly how he died his violent and terrible death. She holds onto the fantasy of him being alive somewhere in order to keep going. It's hard to get old and to realise that you have lost everything to a violent man. That is true of many women I know.

We bonded over that, she and I, over the violence that men do, the violence that they often get away with for their whole lives.

'If they do return, you just tell them the truth, Mary. They must know most of it anyway. Now you get some rest. Maybe a nip of whisky in your tea will help you sleep,' I told her.

'Yes, yes, Caroline, you're right,' she replied and I hoped that she felt better after she put down the phone.

Now as I stare out at the street, I see the front door open and watch as Amanda comes out of her house.

'Why are you even still awake?' I murmur.

Amanda looks straight at me and I sit back in my chair quickly even though I know she can't see me sitting here in the dark.

I watch as she crosses over the road and goes to speak to the police officers in the car. She is holding an empty glass dish in her hand for some reason. When she's done speaking to the police officers, she walks over to Gemma's house where I see her ring the bell.

What on earth can she want with Gemma?

THIRTY

Amanda

She leaves the kitchen, going to her bedroom, the tea forgotten as she gets onto her bed and shuffles back until she's sitting against the headboard.

The article some anonymous person has sent her is from 2012.

The name of the 'wife' in the article – 'Wife Acquitted of Husband's Murder' – is not given. Instead, the journalist has used a pseudonym to discuss the case. She reads it through twice, struggling to understand what it would have to do with anything going on now.

It could be about Caroline or Mary, or really anyone else in the street. Or could it even be someone in the neighbourhood she lived in only a couple of weeks ago?

The neighbourhood where Mike died. Where Jordan was trapped.

Mentally she goes through all her neighbours that she knows, dismissing the two couples who have very young children and the mother and son who live next door because that seems impossible. But Mike is dead and Jordan is missing so nothing is really impossible, is it? Amanda never spoke to any of her neighbours at home really. She was always conscious of keeping her distance. Could someone who lives in the street have broken into their house and hurt Mike, taken Jordan? The possibilities and questions are endless.

She leans back against her headboard and reads it once more.

And then she blows up the picture that accompanies the article, trying to figure out who it is. It's a woman with her head down, one arm up to shield her face. Who is it?

She texts back:

Why have you sent this to me?

But she receives no reply.

Using Google she types in variations of 'wife acquitted' and the date, trying to find the original article, which should surely be somewhere.

She clicks her way through one page after another and is startled to find it's nearly 10 p.m. She looks up from her phone, stretching the crick in her neck. She should get some sleep.

But she knows she won't be able to sleep, so she looks down at her phone again, clicks through to the next page, and there it is, the whole article. And then she finds another article about the same case, and this time, the woman, whose identity has once again been protected with the use of a pseudonym, is not pictured. But now Amanda needs to know who this is about.

She gets off the bed and grabs her shoes. She should call the detective but what would he say? How can this case have anything to do with her son being missing and Mike being dead?

And yet she has to know. Who sent her this? She could go

and ask Caroline, who will be more than willing to help, she's sure.

There is the problem of the police car in the street outside her house. Is she allowed to leave, to go and talk to a neighbour, or will they stop her?

Going into her kitchen, she grabs an empty casserole dish. Will the police officers in the car believe she is returning a dish after ten at night?

She grabs her keys and tentatively opens her front door, then she looks over at Caroline's house but it's in darkness. Mary seems to be asleep as well. Only one house still has lights on and that's Gemma's. She and Gemma have never even had a conversation but she needs to talk to someone. She'll talk to Gemma. Maybe she knows something. Those three are always talking together, drinking tea and gossiping while they do so, no doubt. If there really was a wife around here accused of killing her husband, Gemma would know as much as Mary or Caroline would.

Deciding to tackle things head on, she goes over to the police car and taps on the window. Two young men are sitting inside and when they open the window, a warm fug of fried food smells wafts out, making Amanda feel nauseous. 'I just need to give this back to Gemma,' she says, showing them the dish in her hand as she points to Gemma's house. One young police officer, whose ears stick out from his head, looks to the other and then he turns back to her and nods. She smiles, so they relax. They are not sure what to do. She's not under arrest but she is under suspicion. 'I won't be long.' *Should I show them the article? Would they know what it's about? Would they be able to find out right now because I need to know right now.*

'Okay,' says one of the young men. 'Please go directly back to your house afterwards.'

Amanda nods and she walks over to Gemma's house.

With her phone in one hand and the dish in the other, she

rings Gemma's bell and waits. The air is warm, the sky filled with stars and the brightness of the nearly full moon. It's a beautiful night, a night to be admired and enjoyed, but Amanda is numb with terror and despair. Will she ever be able to admire a beautiful night again? How do you survive without your child?

She thinks of Mike's mother, who is over eighty and lives in a nursing home. Who will tell her that her son is gone?

The door opens and Amanda realises she has interrupted Gemma mid-workout. Her hair is tied back and plastered to her skull and rivulets of sweat run from her neck down into her ample cleavage. Even sweating, the woman looks like a Barbie doll. Amanda could never imagine having the energy to work out so late at night but Gemma's kids are away until next week. Gemma must be bubbling with energy all the time without her parental responsibilities. Tonight, both Amanda's children are gone but they are not enjoying a summer camp. One is with a friend and one is missing. *How did I get here?*

'Oh,' says Gemma.

'I'm sorry, we haven't even met yet,' says Amanda. 'I mean, not formally.'

'That's... that's fine... have they found your son?'

'No... no,' she replies, pushing away the thought, 'but do you mind if I ask you something? I didn't mean to interrupt your workout. Sorry.' She holds up the dish. 'The police are watching my house and I...'

Gemma glances out of her front door at the police car and then she steps back inside and takes the dish. 'I understand,' she says.

'Sorry,' says Amanda again, regretting her decision to come over here.

'Oh, don't worry about it... I was done. Just stretching to go and I can stretch while we talk. Come in.'

Amanda follows Gemma into her beautifully styled living

room, where perfectly white sofas sit on a rich blue carpet. Everything is pristine as though no one lives here but Gemma.

'It's easy to keep things tidy while the girls are away,' Gemma says as though reading her mind. 'All I've done is tidy. And work, I mean, I have to work but without kids there's just so much extra time, isn't there?' The woman's eyes shift from side to side and Amanda can see that Gemma is having trouble making eye contact with her. People feel awkward around grief, around people in terrible situations they themselves don't want to be in. A missing child is every mother's nightmare.

She glances around the room, seeing a picture of Gemma on her wedding day – at least it could be Gemma but the woman in the picture has brown hair and a lot fewer curves than Gemma has.

'I treated myself to some plastic surgery when Rod died,' says Gemma as she sees Amanda looking at the photograph, as though people often look at that photo and ask the same questions. 'I guess his life insurance policy and the girls were the best things that bastard left me.' She shrugs and Amanda nods, unsure what to say. She and Gemma have something in common but she has plenty of friends that she has never told the real truth about her marriage to. And would Gemma even want to hear the truth? Probably not. *You spoke to Caroline*, she reminds herself but Caroline felt different, almost like speaking to her mother.

Whatever happened to Gemma in her marriage, the woman seems to have moved on so thoroughly that Amanda cannot even imagine being in her shoes. A widow. Caroline told Amanda that when they had tea together. 'Being a single mother is hard but Gemma is managing since the death of her husband,' Caroline said.

Amanda could see exactly how the woman was managing.

She reminds herself that the police don't want anyone to know about Mike, not until Jordan is found. She cannot say anything to Gemma about his being dead. *Not just dead but murdered.*

Gemma then lies on the floor, lifting one leg to her nose and then the other, and then she contorts herself into a pose, twisting herself sideways. 'What did you want to talk to me about?' she asks.

Amanda takes her phone out, momentarily distracted by how flexible Gemma is and by the fact that she genuinely is stretching in front of her.

'Oh, um... someone, I don't know who, sent me this article and I was going to ask Caroline about it but I think she's asleep. I think it may be about someone, someone on this street. And if it is, I thought you would know who. I'm not sure why someone would have sent it to me now that Jordan is missing. I mean maybe the two aren't connected but...'

'What does the article say?' asks Gemma, lifting her arm up over her head and bending sideways as she focuses on the wall in front of her.

'Um, you can see,' says Amanda.

'Just read it to me,' instructs Gemma as she bends her head to her knees.

Amanda feels awkward, unsure. She really shouldn't have come here with this, and why won't Gemma stop moving?

'Go on,' says Gemma, and Amanda realises that she has backed herself into a corner.

She clears her throat and reads the article aloud.

WIFE ACQUITTED OF HUSBAND'S MURDER

A woman, whose name has been suppressed for legal reasons, has been acquitted of the murder of her husband. All through the trial, the woman, whom the press gallery has called 'Liza', has stated that her husband was very ill and that he was in desperate pain. She has been quoted as saying, 'He made the choice to take his own life. I am guilty of nothing more than leaving his pain medication near the bed.'

A jury of seven men and five women found that 'Liza' could not have known that her husband had the ability to take his own life.

'She was a saint, caring for him until the very end,' a neighbour of 'Liza's' is quoted as saying.

The woman was charged with manslaughter, telling police that her husband 'really wanted' to die. But at the same time, she also confessed that he was 'mostly asleep'.

She is said to have told police, 'His last words to me were that he was tired of living with his pain.'

The public prosecutor has argued that given the man's diminished state, he was incapable of administering the pain medication to himself.

But the defence argued that sometimes, patients close to death rally enough to talk to family and interact in the world.

'Liza' claims she left her husband alone to rush to the chemist for more medication and came home to find him gone. No one in 'Liza's' family came out to support her at her trial, and when asked about this, she said, 'I don't want to talk about it.' She has one daughter who could not be contacted for comment.

'Do you think this is Mary from next door or Caroline?' Amanda asks. 'The person who sent it to me said I should check out this article about my neighbour. The picture is really unclear. I mean, could it be either of them? And why would some anonymous person send this to me?'

Gemma stands up, her stretching forgotten, and takes the phone from Amanda, scanning the article.

'It's probably just rubbish.'

'Do you know how Mary's husband died? Or Caroline's?'

Gemma shrugs. 'No... look, I can't see either of them being

capable of this although Mary does sound a bit mad these days. I think someone is just being cruel, just messing with you.'

'But why?'

Gemma shrugs her shoulders again. 'I have no idea. People are weird. You should go home and get some rest; you need to sleep. You look exhausted. I'm sure Jordan will be back tomorrow. Have the police got any idea where he is?' Before Amanda can answer, Gemma disappears into the kitchen, returning a moment later with a glass of water in her hand. 'Did you want something to drink?' she asks, her gaze everywhere but on Amanda, and Amanda shakes her head.

'So you have no idea who this could be?' Amanda asks again.

'Well, it's not me.' Gemma laughs as though the idea is completely absurd, which Amanda knows it is. Her husband died only two years ago. 'Look, I know that you're going out of your mind and kind of... clutching at straws but what would this have to do with Jordan being missing?'

Amanda feels her shoulders round and she drops her head. Gemma is right. This is just some weird joke, and even if it's not, it has nothing to do with Jordan.

'Someone just scammed you and you're jumping to conclusions,' says Gemma kindly. 'I wouldn't be surprised if the next message you receive is them asking for money if you want to know who the article is about. It's a scam.'

'Right... right, a scam, it must be a scam.' Amanda stands up and walks to Gemma's front door. 'I know it's a bit crazy but I needed to ask. I'll show this to the detective tomorrow anyway. He will be able to find out exactly who it is or if it's just a scam.'

Gemma nods. 'Right, yes, the detective.' Her eyes shift from side to side. 'You should ask him, he'll know if it has anything to do with Jordan, but it doesn't, I'm sure it doesn't.'

'I can't be sure of anything. Two weeks ago, I had a plan to start my life over again and now Mike is...' She bites down on her lip, the words almost escaping.

'Mike is what?' asks Gemma, her blue eyes wide with curiosity.

'Nothing, nothing. Thanks for trying to help,' says Amanda but she cannot help feeling that she needs to get out of the house and away from Gemma.

As she heads back to her house, she wonders why she's wasting her time with this. She should only be thinking about Jordan and finding him.

She can feel the police officers' eyes on her as she makes her way to her house, where she pushes open the front door and then goes inside.

Looking at the message, she sends another text, trying again.

Why have you sent this to me?

But the sender doesn't reply and she wants to fling her phone across the room.

'Where are you?' she whispers into the air. 'Please come home,' she says but she is only answered with silence. Silence and an empty house.

THIRTY-ONE

Caroline

I stare down at the text message that Gemma has just sent me. I watched Amanda go into Gemma's house and I knew it couldn't be good. I watched her come out and glance over at my house and I was so grateful to have the lights off, to be sitting here in the dark, waiting.

Someone sent her the article from 2012

That was all she needed to send.

Tiny pinpricks of panic race around my body.

I am exposed. I am unmasked. I am humiliated. I am caught.

Someone sent Amanda the article? No, I know it was not just *someone*, not just anyone, but a person I know very well, a person I gave all my love to, a person who fought me on everything her whole life. A person who was supposed to be in my life, caring for me as I grew older.

I send the *someone* a text. Perhaps she will be asleep already, perhaps she simply won't answer. Or maybe, just maybe, she will be confused because maybe she is not actually capable of such a terrible betrayal. A tiny flower of hope blooms inside me. No matter how angry she is with me, I'm still her mother. She wouldn't betray me like this, would she? I look down at the words of the text.

Why would you do that? What are you hoping to achieve?

I wait, the sensation of seconds ticking away all through my body as I watch my phone until my daughter replies.

She needed to know who she was living just across the street from.

I don't understand. How did you even get her number? And why would you want to contact her? What on earth would that have to do with this missing child?

It's easy enough to find a mobile number. Her name is everywhere. And I want everyone to know what kind of a person lives in that street. She'll start asking questions and that's a good thing. Maybe she'll show the police and then you'll be exposed and everyone will know what you did. Maybe they'll even open the case again.

You break my heart, Janine. You know he was sick. You know he was violent. You left me alone to care for him myself. And he was ready to go. He made the choice.

He was never violent. He protected me from you my whole life. He was never aggressive and I don't know how you managed to convince the doctors and nurses that he was. I don't know how you got

everyone onside but you're a manipulative psychopath and you need to pay for what you did.

Evil, wicked words. She has flung them at me before, just after her father's death as I struggled through cleaning out his clothes and things, memories assaulting me at every turn. She was supposed to be helping, supposed to be comforting me, but she was just so furious, so enraged and so filled with accusations. She was the one who went to the police, something I will never forgive her for, although I have tried to continue being a mother to her.

You blame me because it's easier than blaming yourself, because you made the choice to go travelling when he was so near the end. You left me to take care of him and now you're sorry and you have blamed me for ten years when the person you should be blaming is yourself.

You're so wicked, so awful, twisting everything around. You told me to go away, you told me to leave. You wanted me gone so you could end his life and there was still a chance that he could recover. The doctors said the chemo was working.

I feel sorry for you, Janine. You are delusional. You had a wonderful childhood and I gave you everything and you insist on misremembering it. And you misremember his illness and death in the same way.

Liar!!!! You hurt me. All you wanted was to control me. And now a child is missing, a child that lives right across the road from you. I hope that poor woman shows the police and that people look into the case again. I hope the press come

back to ask questions and that your whole ugly life is laid bare. You don't deserve to be alive. You're a monster.

The only monster is the monster your father became. And only when you have your own child will you understand how terrible it is to experience this dreadful lack of gratitude.

Well, you'll never know, will you? You will never meet my child or children.

These words catch me by surprise. I know that in her teens, when our relationship strained to breaking point, Janine told me she would never have children in case she became a mother like me. Now she is speaking of having children. Is she pregnant? Does she already have a child?

We haven't spoken for such a long time. I was a good mother. Perhaps my discipline was a bit old-fashioned but Liam was so soft with her. She had him wrapped around her little finger with her smile and her cocked head and the way she said, 'Daddy, please.' I was the one who had to make sure she got to school on time and did her homework, cooked her dinner, made sure she had a shower, and she was a wilful little girl and a worse teenager. I know I only tell people that she got difficult when she became a teenager but the truth is that Janine was always difficult. She needed to be shown the correct way to behave and I disciplined her as I had been disciplined.

In my day, when I was a child, that was the correct way to do things. It is only as time has gone on that people have decided that children don't benefit from a short sharp smack, from a little deprivation, from an understanding that they are not the ones running the house. I am certain that Amanda has never used proper discipline with her son. She probably thought putting him on a time-out was extreme and look what he has become.

Janine is a successful physiotherapist with a lovely husband because she was raised the right way. I didn't get to attend her wedding. I wasn't invited but I saw the pictures on Facebook. She hasn't blocked me and I have never understood why but I think that perhaps she wants me to see that she is happy without me, living her life. It has been over a decade since I got a Mother's Day card or a birthday wish. I, of course, always send her my best. I am a good mother but even a good mother can raise a terrible child.

I believe she simmers in anger over her father's death and she must have been delighted to see the story of the missing boy on the news and to realise that he lived in my street. But she cannot assuage her own guilt by throwing me under the bus.

She has no idea what I went through at the end. No idea and she doesn't want to know because that means she would have to forgive me and that means blaming herself.

I'm not going to accept the police asking me questions again, not going to tolerate the press returning to follow and harass me. I have a new life, a good life, a peaceful one.

For about the tenth time, I wish that Amanda had never come to live here and disturb this quiet street. But she's here now and I'll have to deal with her.

I reply to Gemma's text.

All that was a long time ago and I won't tolerate my life being subject to scrutiny again. I'm sure you understand.

She's talking about going to the police, about asking them about it.

I feel my breath catch in my throat. This has all gone too far now.

That's not going to happen. It better not happen, I reply.

I go through my messages from Janine before deleting them all. I don't need that poison on my phone.

I have a life here and I'm going to protect that life.

My phone rings and I know it will be Gemma, reassuring me of her silence because she worries about everything I know about her. Good, she should worry. When the call is done, I glance out of the window. The police car is still in the street but there are ways through the back gardens. We are all connected here on the curve of the cul-de-sac. My garden is next to Gemma's garden and that is next to Mary's garden, which is right next door to Amanda. We can easily move between houses without being seen.

I message Gemma once more.

You need to go and talk to her. And then you need to come over here. We can sort all this out. Use the back gardens.

Gemma replies almost instantly, as though she has been waiting for my instruction.

Okay.

'Good,' I mutter and I go into my bedroom, donning my gown and lying down on my bed, waiting for what is to come.

THIRTY-TWO

Amanda

Amanda is lying on Jordan's bed, which is still unmade from the last time he slept in it. It has his particular smell that she just wants to be near to.

A tapping sound like someone knocking on the window makes her sits up. Did she really just hear that? She strains to listen again, sure that she imagined it, but there it is again, a sound like someone knocking on glass. She gets off the bed and goes to the window, flinging open the curtains, but there's nothing to see and then she hears the sound again. It's coming from the living room, where there are sliding glass doors that lead to the back garden. *Jordan. He's home, he's home.* Waves of relief crash through her because this is over, finally over. *But Mike is still dead. I can't think about that now.*

As she rushes out of the room, she stubs her toe on the edge of the door and she bends over, pain slicing through her as she grabs her toe and squeezes.

She imagines Jordan will be hungry and tired and she curses herself for not having something on the stove, something to feed him. She should have made lasagne and kept it in the oven, kept it warm all night because he loves lasagne. When she is upright again, she walks slowly so that she doesn't hurt herself again.

But it's not Jordan. Standing at the sliding glass doors in her back garden is Gemma. Amanda's heart sinks, her throbbing toe reminding her of her moment of hope.

Limping, she moves over to the doors and pulls them open.

'Um, there's something I need to tell you, something about Caroline.' Gemma's hair is still tied back and she is still in her workout clothes. She looks nervous, unsure, as she moves from one foot to the other. The rush of relief drains from Amanda's body, replaced by a terrible despair. Why is Gemma here and what could she possibly need to say? Exhaustion tugs at her, enticing her to bed and the possibility of a few hours of sleep. But Gemma must be here for a reason.

Amanda steps back to let her in, her arms folded across her chest. 'What do you have to tell me?'

Gemma looks around, swallows. 'This is... nice.'

'Gemma,' says Amanda, her patience quickly running out, 'it's very late. I'm sure you're here for a reason. And why come around the back?'

'I didn't want the police to know I was here. And I just... I don't want to cause any trouble but I thought about your son and I just... I have to say something.' She wrings her hands together.

'What?' demands Amanda. 'What do you have to say about anything to do with Jordan, what are you talking about?' Her voice is high, harsh, but she's struggling with her devastation that it was not her son knocking on the glass doors.

'Caroline is the woman in the article.' The words burst from Gemma's lips, a balloon of truth popping into the air. 'And I don't think her husband did kill himself. I mean, I never knew him but she's told me stories...'

'Stories?' questions Amanda.

Gemma perches on the edge of the sofa so that Amanda sits down as well.

'He was very domineering, not violent but unkind, cruel really, at least that's what she told me when I moved here, after I got to know her. I told her about Rod, because he hurt me, just like Mike... your husband hurt you.'

'You don't know anything about my marriage, Gemma.' They have all been talking about her, gossiping about her. No one can be trusted. She should never have spoken to Caroline.

'Caroline told me... Look, when I told Caroline about Rod, she confessed that she had experienced abuse herself from Liam, after he got sick. Cancer spread to his brain and he was vicious and violent. I mean I'm not sure if that's the truth. I think her daughter has a very different version of things. Caroline says that Janine is almost delusional but I just—'

'So she killed him? You think she actually killed him?'

Gemma shrugs. 'I don't know. I'm not sure but I do know...' She stops speaking and looks around the room as though someone else might appear.

'We're alone,' says Amanda.

Gemma stands up and comes over to Amanda, leans down and whispers in her ear, 'Caroline hates men, hates them.'

'So she...' begins Amanda but then she stops to think about Jordan, who was a problem to the street, mean and nasty, keeping people up and rude to everyone. And now Jordan is missing. But Jordan's not a man, he's just a boy.

'Oh God,' says Amanda and she leaps up. 'Are you saying she's done something to Jordan?'

Gemma shakes her head. 'No... I mean I don't think so but I...' She smooths her hair back, her gaze on the floor. 'She's just not nice, Amanda, she collects secrets and then she uses them to blackmail people and she's just not nice,' she looks up at Amanda, her face twisting, 'and I'm sick of her telling everyone what to do. I'm sick of being told what to do. I had that with Rod, I don't need it with Caroline.'

'Look, I don't understand what you're trying to say here, Gemma. If you don't like Caroline, why don't you just stay out of her way?'

'You don't understand,' says Gemma, her voice rising in pitch. 'She knows everything about me, about my marriage and the things Rod did and she'll...'

Amanda stands and pushes her hands through her hair, frustration making her impatient. 'Why are you here, Gemma? Do you actually believe Caroline has hurt my son? Do you believe that she knows where he is? Because his backpack was found at my home, where we used to live... so what does that have to do with Caroline?'

Gemma's eyes widen, and her face pales. 'They found his backpack? Why didn't... why didn't anyone say? Like on the news or something. I've been watching the news.'

Amanda wants to lash out at the woman. Why does she care that no one told her? Why would anyone tell her anything at all? She's never spoken to Jordan, and Amanda is sure the woman dislikes her son as much as Caroline and Mary do. She doesn't owe Gemma an explanation. She owes Gemma nothing at all.

'The police don't want to discuss it,' she snaps, gratified that Gemma cowers at the admonishment.

Then she sighs. 'Gemma, you came here for a reason – do you think Caroline is somehow involved with Jordan going missing?'

'I...' Gemma shakes her head. 'I'm not saying anything at all, I just thought that you should know that she's not always to be trusted, that's all I wanted to say.'

Amanda studies Gemma, watches the way the woman can't meet her gaze, sees how she is fidgeting with the chunky ring on her finger.

'And you want to say something else, don't you?'

Gemma nods. 'She saw you.'

'Saw me?'

'Last night. Caroline saw you leaving late at night. She saw you and if you show the police the article, she will tell them that you left the kids alone.'

'Oh God.' Amanda pushes her fingers against her burning eyes.

Gemma is silent for a moment and then she whispers, 'She's such a bitch. She watches everyone, all the time.'

'The police know anyway, Gemma. I had to tell them.'

'Oh, well then, I suppose... you don't have to worry.'

'I absolutely have to worry. I shouldn't have left them alone and now I think I left only Kiera. Jordan was already gone when I left. It's a miracle that nothing happened to her.'

'Where did you go?' asks Gemma, cocking her head to one side.

'It doesn't... matter.' Amanda's dream comes back to her, a flash of her staring down at her hands covered in blood, but it was only a dream, just a dream. And then she thinks about what Gemma has just said. 'How long has Caroline been watching my house? Did she see when Jordan left? Did she actually see him leave?'

Gemma's eyes dart from side to side. 'I didn't ask her about that,' she says, her voice rising slightly. The woman is not even trying to conceal that she's lying. She's lying about a lot of things, but just how much, Amanda can't be sure.

'If she saw him leave, why didn't she say anything? Why didn't she tell the police?' asks Amanda, fury coursing through her. Maybe if Caroline had said something, Jordan would be home right now.

'She's... Caroline has her own agenda.'

'What does that mean?' demands Amanda, folding her arms across her chest again.

Gemma offers her another shrug and Amanda clenches her fist, the urge to deliver a quick slap to Gemma's perfect cheek almost overwhelming her. Why won't she give her a straight answer?

'I'm going to talk to her right now,' she says, not caring how late it is, not caring if she wakes Caroline.

'You shouldn't do that,' warns Gemma, 'and the police are out front.'

'I'll go and ask them to talk to her then.' Amanda moves towards the front door. Gemma grabs her arm.

'No, don't.'

Amanda shakes her off. 'Why? If Caroline knows something, the best people to talk to her are the police.'

'Amanda, wait,' she says forcefully, 'trust me when I tell you that if Caroline knows something, anything, and you send the police to talk to her, you'll get nothing. She fooled the police once, didn't she? If you want to know something, you need to go to her and ask her yourself.'

'Does Caroline know where Jordan is?' hisses Amanda, stepping right up to Gemma, getting in the woman's face.

Gemma drops her head. 'I don't know, but if she does, she won't tell you anything if you send the police.'

Amanda hesitates. Is Gemma telling the truth? What if Caroline really does know something and refuses to speak to the police? What if Jordan is out there somewhere and Caroline knows where he is and she keeps that to herself because she's angry about the police coming to speak to her?

'Fine,' she says, through gritted teeth. 'I'll speak to her, I'll ask her.'

'Okay, we can go around the back, follow me.'

Amanda looks around for some shoes but can't see where she put her sandals, and Gemma is already walking out the door. Panicked, she just follows her into the cool air of the back garden, the grass prickly underneath her bare feet, her toe throbbing from where it was stubbed.

Feeling stupid, she follows Gemma across Mary's back garden, moving in the shadows, and then across Gemma's back garden, where the lawn is manicured and the flower beds neat and tidy.

Each garden has a small fence between it and the next garden, small enough to scramble over. Amanda wishes for shoes but it's too late now. As they make it into Caroline's garden with its little wooden bridge and white pebbles everywhere, Amanda walks slowly, the pebbles pushing into her feet. She has also left her phone at home, something that she curses herself for.

They make their way to the door that opens on to the garden and Gemma knocks, once, twice and then a few more times. Finally, Amanda steps forward and pounds on the glass.

A light goes on somewhere in the house and then the kitchen light is turned on and Caroline is standing there, a baseball bat in her hand, her body covered in a lumpy blue dressing gown and her hair in curlers. She doesn't look like the kind of woman who could murder her ill husband but she may just know something about Jordan, especially if she's always watching everything going on in the cul-de-sac.

When she moved here Amanda knew that this was not a nice place to live, but she had come for a reason. She hoped that Mike would not come here and that if he did, he would be wary of making a scene.

And now she is paying the price for trying to control an uncontrollable situation.

'My goodness,' says Caroline as she opens the sliding door, 'what on earth is going on? It's very late.'

'Gemma told me that you know something about what's happened to Jordan,' snaps Amanda, her patience running out.

'I didn't...' begins Gemma.

'Heavens, Gemma, why are you making up stories?' She rolls her eyes and smiles as though this is funny.

'Caroline, if you know where my son went, if you saw him leave, you need to tell me now.'

'Calm down,' says Caroline softly and she steps back to let them into the kitchen. 'Why on earth would you think I know anything?' She is looking at Gemma as she speaks and Amanda wants to yell and scream because she's not in the mood for this shit.

'I saw that article about you. Someone sent it to me and I think it's because you know something about Jordan. I'm showing it to the detectives tomorrow. I don't know how it's connected but someone wanted me to know that you're capable of...' she hesitates because suddenly, faced with Caroline in her dressing gown, it all seems quite preposterous, 'murder,' she finishes, looking down at her dirty feet, staining Caroline's white kitchen floor.

And Caroline bursts out laughing.

THIRTY-THREE

Caroline

'I don't know who you think you are,' I say, chuckling some more, 'but I know you left your children alone and that's probably when your child ran away. I have no idea what article you are talking about. You sound unhinged, Amanda, are you feeling all right?'

I glance over at Gemma, who is watching us, chewing at her fingernails, something she gave up long ago. She has told Amanda that the article was about me, which I knew would send Amanda straight here. I can't have the woman showing that to the police. I simply will not tolerate my personal business becoming fodder for the press again and the last thing I need is for the police to decide they need to look at me more closely.

Amanda's mouth closes and she blinks quickly. I can see she feels ridiculous now, coming over here with accusations about nothing in particular, but she is a problem. I can see that she will be a problem. The police knowing about the article is not my issue. I was acquitted. I did nothing wrong. What I can't stand is the scrutiny that will come with its exposure. Questions may be asked about the other things that have happened on this street. The vultures of the press will circle and I will be exposed as will Mary and Gemma, my friends. All those years ago, I received hate mail from strangers. Who knows what could happen today with all the dregs of humanity trolling social media. I cannot be exposed again. That's what my ungrateful daughter wants. All I want is to be left alone.

I wanted to help Amanda and maintain the peace in our street. And now everything is a bit of a mess thanks to Gemma's stupidity, and it's going to be very hard to clean up thanks to my vengeful, bitter daughter.

Collecting other people's secrets is a passion of mine. That's why I'm always watching what's going on outside my house. It means I am able to help others as well so everyone wins. Sometimes people need help, even when they don't ask for it. I knew Gemma needed help. And I know Amanda also needed help.

'Please, Caroline,' says Amanda, 'I just want to know where he is.' Her brown eyes fill with tears and I almost feel sorry for her – almost but not quite. She is making my kitchen floor dirty and my fingers itch for a mop to clean it up.

'You know, this was a lovely street before you moved here. We had gotten it just the way we wanted to, hadn't we, Gemma?'

Gemma doesn't reply, instead looking away as a flush touches her cheeks.

It's easy for her to forget now that he's been gone for two years, easy for her to just pretend that what happened never happened, but I'm not one to let someone get away with pretending. Reality is reality and it must be acknowledged.

'Wait here,' I say and I leave Amanda and Gemma standing in the kitchen while I go to my bedroom, where I take off my gown and remove my curlers. I am dressed underneath. I knew Gemma would lead Amanda here. I told her to.

When I return, Gemma and Amanda are still standing there and I glance down at my floor, irritated that no effort has been made to clean it. I hand Amanda a pair of old slippers. Who leaves the house without shoes? Ridiculous woman.

I really had a wonderful plan for tonight and now it's all ruined. It's ruined because Janine sent the article to Amanda and she went straight to Gemma to ask questions. I suppose I should be grateful that Amanda didn't go straight to the police although detectives are unlikely to have turned up here until tomorrow and by then everything would be as it should be.

Now I need to deal with this situation. I sigh as Luna comes to greet our visitors, winding herself around Gemma's legs but staying away from Amanda. Neither Luna nor I are fond of tears and hysteria. It's better to remain calm and in control. More things get done that way.

'Sit down, Amanda,' I say as she and Gemma follow me into my living room. And when she starts to shake her head, I push her towards the sofa. 'Sit down or you'll never see that wretched child again.' I bare my teeth and her mouth gapes open as she realises exactly what I have just said.

'You know... you know where he is,' she stutters. 'Tell me. Tell me right now. I'll call...' She looks around her frantically. She hasn't brought her phone. 'You have to tell me; you have to tell me.' Her voice rises towards hysteria.

'Of course,' I say, soothing her now. I just need a moment, to buy some time before she decides to do something ridiculous like rush at me, hit me, or even run off and make this mess even worse. This was not supposed to happen, was not supposed to be my problem, but I involved Gemma and bless her, the woman is not the brightest.

Amanda needs to remain sitting down until I am ready. I turn around and open a drawer in a buffet I have in the living room. It's an old timber piece with intricate carving. I inherited it from my mother and I have treasured it ever since, making sure to polish it with a special oil once a month. I take out a knife, large and silver with a smooth blade. I'm not going to do anything with it but I feel it will be helpful to have in case Amanda feels the need to get physical.

When she sees the knife, Amanda sits back further on the sofa, her brown eyes widening.

'Now.' I point the knife in her direction. 'I feel that I should explain. I married a man who was very different to my father, kind and loving, too sweet really and too easy to control, but it's what I wanted. I thought that if I chose the right man, my life would be so much better than my mother's had been. I never counted on an ungrateful child and my Janine was so very difficult. And I never anticipated Liam getting ill and all his festering hate for me, all his rage against me, coming up and making him so very...' I wave the knife around, trying to find the right way to explain things but I can't come up with anything except, 'difficult.'

'Caroline, please, I'm begging you. If you know where Jordan is, please tell me,' whispers Amanda, making sure to keep her voice low, lest she upset me. I offer her a smile.

'All in good time, my dear. When Liam died, Janine blamed me, even got the police involved if you can believe that, such an ungrateful girl. But I was cleared of any wrongdoing and I moved here. Mary was my first real friend. And her story was so sad. Do you know Mary's story?' I ask and then without letting Amanda say anything I continue, 'Of course you don't. You've been quite involved with yourself and that would have been fine if your son had not brought such disruption to our little cul-de-sac.' I sigh as I think about Mary.

'Her husband killed her son. Her son was such a good boy, growing up kind and sweet and so protective of his mother. He was only eighteen when he got between his father and mother. The way Mary tells it, one of them was going to die that night and unfortunately, it was her son.' I think about

Mary's little fantasy about James. It's guilt. Mothers are supposed to protect their children and not the other way around. Dan went to jail so at least he was out of Mary's life, but she's been alone ever since. I know that James wasn't exactly sweet when he was a teenager. He was turning into his father as they all eventually do, hurting his mother and then apologising and then hurting her again. Mary never wanted to reveal that bit of information but we have been friends a long time and on nights when we shared a drink or two, things came out, things that I have remembered and held on to.

'I don't—' says Amanda and I wave the knife at her again, needing her to be quiet. I have a feeling that if she could just understand what can happen when bad men go unchallenged, then she will understand and accept what's happened now. She has suffered at the hands of her husband and I can see that she was on her way to suffering at the hands of her son as well.

'Dan went to prison and died there and Mary was left alone, totally and completely alone. She's never recovered. She had her work to distract her when she was younger but since she retired and as she gets older, she resides in a fantasy world where her son is alive and that makes me so angry for her, so very angry. Bad men need to be stopped.

'That was the problem for Gemma as well, wasn't it, Gemma?' I glance at Gemma, who nods obediently.

'You brought Amanda over here to tell her about my crimes but you didn't think to mention your own, did you?'

Gemma drops her head.

'Rod was a terrible man, a vicious man who beat Gemma and who was already turning his anger on his lovely girls. I couldn't let that happen and Gemma was so grateful when he died. I mean, look at her, she has positively blossomed.' I gesture towards Gemma's ample chest.

'You're not going to get away with this,' says Amanda, her

fists clenched. 'The police are outside and all I have to do is open my mouth and scream and they will come in here...'

I move over to her, lean down and hold the knife close to one of her pretty eyes. 'I dare you,' I say and take some pleasure at the tears that spill onto her cheeks.

'I just want my son, please tell me where he is.' More tears appear. 'The detectives will be back at dawn,' she says, her voice shuddering with emotion.

'This will all be over by dawn,' I say with a smile.

'Caroline, this needs to stop,' snaps Gemma and I point the knife at her. She shrinks back and I indicate the sofa so she sits down.

'You just sit there and keep quiet, Gemma. You've done more than enough to mess this up. All you were supposed to do was get rid of that stupid man so that Amanda could take her family back home and leave us all in peace.'

Amanda gasps and looks at Gemma.

Gemma's eyes fill with silly tears as her cheeks burn red. 'I did what you told me. But he was... Mike was... he was too strong. He pushed me away and then he opened that room. I didn't know he was in there.' She turns to look at Amanda. 'I promise you I didn't know Jordan was there but I couldn't... I had to do what she said. You don't understand, Amanda. I had to do what she said. She has recordings of me talking about what happened to Rod and she'll... I can't lose my girls... I can't.'

'You knew... you saw... you saw Jordan there, you went to my house, you killed Mike?' Amanda is shaking her head as she tries to understand what Gemma is saying. I play with the point of the knife, enjoying the little show as I plan my next move.

'I had to do what Caroline said,' whines Gemma, 'and I couldn't leave Jordan there, he knew, he saw me.'

'You bitch,' Amanda screams, throwing herself at Gemma, who rears back in shock. I step towards them and use my knife to slice across Amanda's cheek, just a nick really, just a small reminder of who's in charge here. She sits back, stunned and clutching her face, blood pooling over her fingers, and I wave the knife at her, warning her not to repeat her behaviour.

'You would have been so happy, Amanda. That was the plan. Your horrible husband disappears as all horrible husbands should and you would have gone home and taken your troublesome son with you. You would never have stayed here if Mike was dead and we knew that. But then, in a dreadful coincidence, you went and messed it all up by leaving the house on the same night we planned to eliminate your husband problem. We didn't know where you'd gone. And we had no idea that your son had also chosen that night to meet his father. You should have known where your son was and what he was doing. I have no idea how a mother can pay so little attention to her children.'

'I don't understand,' says Amanda and I can see that I still have more explaining to do.

'After you drove away from your former home, Gemma went in there, ringing the bell and dragging your husband out of bed. He must have assumed it was you and that you had come to get your son because he hid the child in that room in the study. He was very surprised to see you at the door, wasn't he, Gemma?'

Gemma nods. 'I told him I had to talk to him about you and Kiera and he took me to the study and then I told...' Gemma shakes her head and then covers her mouth with her hand, her face a ghostly white. She takes a deep breath and turns to Amanda. 'I told him that he had no right to hurt you and he was so...' Gemma waves her hand as I wait patiently for her to explain it to Amanda. I know what happened but it's important that Amanda knows that Gemma did her a huge favour, at my behest of course. 'He asked me who I thought I was and he told me that he didn't need some...' Gemma hesitates and takes a ragged breath, 'some idiot Barbie doll interfering in his life. We were standing in his study and I had my back to the wall and my bag on my shoulder and he looked at me and it was that... that look, you know? You know, Amanda, don't you? The look they get when they're going to hit you?'

'I don't... you're lying, you're...' Amanda shakes her head and I feel frustration building up inside me.

'Just finish the story, Gemma,' I say. I need Gemma to tell Amanda everything she did because then Amanda knows and I know and I have one more of Gemma's secrets to hold on to for her.

Gemma turns away from Amanda. 'He came towards me and he didn't know I had the hammer in my bag.' Her voice is low, emotionless, as though she now just needs the words to be said. 'I hit him and then he staggered away, towards the bookcase, and pulled on the book and he fell and I hit him again.' Gemma stops speaking and looks at me. 'Is that what you wanted, Caroline? I've confessed to a terrible crime. Is that what you needed me to do?'

She is infuriated with me. Angry for making her do what was necessary and angry for making her confess it. But I feel like we're all just a little closer now. Three women who needed to be rid of their terrible husbands. The world would be a much better place if there were more people like me trying to sort things out but alas, I can't be everywhere.

'Caroline,' says Amanda, standing up and throwing a look of deep disgust and hatred at Gemma, who shrinks into her seat. She was never cut out for this sort of thing and I knew that but I helped her get rid of her revolting husband and she owed me. I was horrified when she turned up here close to dawn with the limp boy in tow, her body bowed under his weight, sweating and panting as she struggled to hold him.

'He was hiding in the house and I hit him with the hammer, I didn't know what else to do,' she cried. And then of course it became my problem.

'You sit down,' I tell Amanda but she takes a step towards me.

'Caroline,' she says, baring her teeth at me, 'take me to my son or I swear I will kill you. You may have a knife but you have my son and I will tear you apart if I have to.' She takes another step towards me and I stare at her as it occurs to me that some women are awful as well and need to be dealt with. Janine is awful but she has run away. Amanda is also awful and she's a bad mother who let her son drive us all crazy and then left her other child alone in a house at night for hours.

'Come with me.' I gesture with the knife and Amanda begins to walk, her fists clenched and her body rigid.

'Come, Gemma,' I instruct and Gemma stands because she has no idea what else to do, silly girl.

'Come, come,' I tell them both and we walk towards my basement door, to where all my jars of pickles are stored. To where I store everything that should be kept away from the light.

THIRTY-FOUR

Amanda

Amanda walks in the direction Caroline is pointing with the knife; Gemma follows her.

'Just over there to the basement door. You'll see him soon enough.'

She cannot believe that this is actually happening, that she is here in this mad woman's house where her son probably is. Is Jordan here? Is Caroline lying? She is obviously completely insane and Amanda cannot even contemplate the idea that she was involved in Gemma's husband's death. Surely this is all one colossal joke. How could she have moved here to get away from violence only to find herself surrounded by violence again? Who are these women? How has no one realised what's going on here?

'Before you came, it was just us girls and women,' says Caroline as they stop in front of her basement door, 'and it was so pleasant. I know that teenage girls can be difficult but then Gemma has the money to send hers away when they get too...' Caroline hesitates, 'mouthy.' She smiles.

'They're good girls,' whispers Gemma.

'Of course they are,' agrees Caroline, 'and you keep them in line because if you don't, the police may have to hear the truth about Rod's accident, and no one wants that, do they?'

She opens the door, using a key hanging around her neck, still managing to hold on to the knife. Amanda wonders what it would take to grab the knife and the key and she turns to look at Gemma, to signal her to help, but Gemma looks down and then away. Amanda knows that the two of them could easily wrest the knife away from Caroline.

The basement door opens and the fusty smell of damp and old clothes wafts up on cool air.

'He's down there,' says Caroline, 'go on.'

Amanda takes a step forward and then stops. 'Wait,' she says, because what if this is all just some weird trick? What if Jordan is not down there at all? 'Is there a light?'

Caroline steps towards her. 'Not for you.' Amanda feels hands on her back and she knows they are Gemma's hands because she can feel a ragged fingernail scratching through her thin top. She braces her body but Gemma's push is strong and sure and then Amanda is tumbling down the stairs.

The last words she hears before her head hits the cement floor of the basement are, 'Well done, Gemma.'

THIRTY-FIVE

Caroline

I slam the door shut. 'See,' I say to Gemma, 'I told you it would be easy.'

Gemma nods but her hands go to her mouth again, her teeth biting down nervously on a nail. 'You need to stop that,' I tell her. 'It ruins your lovely hands.'

'What are you going to do?' asks Gemma, and I sigh because I hate having to explain everything.

'I'm going to let nature and time take its course. I may have to go down there and do something about the smell in the next few days but I know how to handle that.'

'And what if the police come?' she asks, her voice high-pitched with fear.

'But the police are not going to come because when they come in the morning, they will discover that Amanda has left to look for her boy or run away because she killed her own child. They will assume she must have snuck out at some point during the night. She didn't even take her car because she didn't want to alert the police outside her door, but she took some clothes and her phone.'

'This is so wrong,' moans Gemma, 'we should get the boy medical help, we need to let Amanda out and call an ambulance and—'

'Just stop,' I spit, pointing the knife at her. 'If my dreadful daughter had never sent her that article, we would have been able to place the boy somewhere in the bush tonight. We found the perfect spot yesterday. They would have found him in the morning, and this would all have been done. And what's more, if you had simply shoved him back into that safe room and left him there, it would no longer be a problem at all. You messed up and now this needs to be fixed.'

I cannot even count the number of ways that Gemma has messed this up. She may have told Amanda that she only went to talk to Mike, but she went there to get rid of him. It was the least I could do for Amanda. And I can't deny that sending Gemma off to do my bidding filled me with a secret thrill. I have a fantasy that I would never tell anyone but it's an idea that makes me smile: a network of women, all getting rid of the awful men in the world. Peace would be the order of the day and all the violence that men do would disappear.

Gemma was very reluctant to go and deal with Amanda's husband. If I didn't know better, I would say that she was actually attracted to the man. He is – or was – certainly good-looking but surface polish usually conceals a ragged inside. The man needed to die. She called me on the way there, begging me to just let this go. 'We can all survive the next few months,' she told me as she drove to Amanda's house, but I wasn't having that. 'Get rid of him,' I told Gemma. Really, I was only trying to help Amanda. I try to do good in the world, but because it is necessary for me to involve other people, everything gets mucked up. It all would have been fine if there was just one less dreadful man in the world today but Gemma saw the boy and panicked and here we are.

'Caroline, I don't want...' begins Gemma and I know she is going to tell me that she doesn't want to do any of the things I have instructed her to do, and really it is quite tiresome.

'You can sort this out for me because you owe me and you will never stop owing me,' I snap. 'You put the pills in Rod's drink so he would lose control and then you ran so he would chase you. All I did was hit him with my car. It was your plan, Gemma, remember that. Now go. And remember to take the SIM card out of Amanda's phone and break it, we don't want the police tracing it.'

Gemma's face pales and a hand goes to her mouth, frustrating me, and I slap it away before she can bite down on a nail. 'Stop being so pathetic,' I command. 'Go and do what I told you to do or it will be too late and then we will both be going to jail.' I walk back to my living room and twitch the net curtain slightly. The police car is still there, the occupants inside unconcerned with what is going on at my house. 'Go now, go back the way you came, take the phone and some clothes and hide them in your house. Hide it well, Gemma, and when the police leave, we'll dispose of all of it. And then get into bed and just go to sleep. I'll sort everything else out.' If Gemma keeps Amanda's things, it will be one more little secret to add to my collection, something I can use in the future if I need to.

Gemma hustles herself out of the house to the back garden and I watch her until she is in her own garden, walking towards Mary's. Mary is a sound sleeper and it's a good thing none of us have a dog to bark and wake everyone up.

I'm sure she'll screw it up in some way but police are notoriously stupid and it will take them months to figure it out. The good thing about the basement is that its walls are thick. There is a small window but I don't think it would be very easy to hear someone scream for help. But it's still a good idea to make sure that Amanda and her boy remain silent.

Sighing, I glance down at my dirty kitchen floor and then I get out the mop. I do hate to go to bed when the house is a mess. Some bleach has soon cleaned everything away and the floor sparkles again as though I never had my barefoot visitor.

I think that I should, perhaps, consider moving now. I've been here for some time, and I know that my house would fetch a good sum of money. There are so many other streets in Australia where I could be of help to the women suffering with terrible men. I will miss Mary. She helped me when I really needed help. But I am sure she will be fine. I have suffered for this life, for my contentment, and I'm not going to let anyone take it from me. Gemma will be glad if I leave, and I will, of course, check on Mary until she dies, but she can't be long for this world.

Humming as I make my way to my bedroom, I begin to contemplate where else I could go. I do need to wait for the basement to be cleared, of course. But that won't take long. It won't take long at all.

THIRTY-SIX

Amanda

She opens her eyes in the dark, her head immediately throbbing intensely with each beat of her heart.

The smell of mould, of damp darkness, is all around her and as she moves, she can feel the cold of the cement floor she is lying on.

If you leave me, you'll regret it. I promise you; you'll regret it.

His words come back to her in a rush, and adrenalin allows her to move her aching body into a sitting position. Even without touching her skin she can feel bruises forming everywhere from her tumble down the stairs.

She needs some light, needs to be able to see, but she doesn't have her phone. She closes her eyes, sees it sitting on the coffee table in her living room, sees the ugly green case she uses to protect it, chosen because it's so easy to spot in her bag or on a table or a counter. But she left without it, in a panicked rush, following Gemma without even stopping for shoes. This street was supposed to be a safe place for her and her children, a new street in a new suburb where they couldn't be found. But that's not the whole truth, that's not the only reason she came here. She has put herself and her needs first and now her children will be lost forever. A soft whimper escapes her but she swallows down anything else. She needs to survive this.

In an effort to concentrate, she stills her body, her arms hugging her knees. Blinking, she can see that it is not entirely dark, that there is light coming in from a tiny window. It's still dark outside but the moon is bright in a cloudless sky. How long has she been out? When will dawn and more police arrive, and will they find her, find them? Is he here? Or is he gone? If she screams, will the police in their squad car hear her and come and save her? And how fast would they get here? Fast enough to stop Caroline?

She uses her hand, touches around her head, feels matted stickiness in her hair. Blood. She must have hit her head on the stairs or the floor.

As her eyes adjust, she sees shapes, recognises a chair, a table, a stack of boxes, a rack with jars, lots of jars that she knows are pickled vegetables. She shivers with a skin-crawling fear that there may be any number of small creatures down here with her. But she is not what matters. She moves her head around the room, looking for him, seeking her child. The child who was so angry with her that he ran away, home to his awful father only to be hurt by a stranger who was coerced there by a psychopath. That's what Caroline is. It doesn't matter how she explains the things she does to herself, that's what she is.

'Jordan,' she whispers because she knows that Caroline may be listening and she does not want her to know she is awake and moving.

'Jordan,' she whispers again and then louder, 'Jordan.' But there is no reply. She waits a beat, waiting to hear the word 'mum'.

Shuffling along so that she doesn't bump into anything, she moves towards the window so that she can use the light. More shapes appear, a rocking chair, a chest of drawers, a pile of clothing.

And then she sees him.

He is on his side, curled up small. He is not moving.

In a second, she is next to him. 'Baby, baby, wake up,' she cries as she touches him. But he doesn't move at all. She shakes him, needing him to move, but there is nothing. Gemma hit him with a hammer just like she hit Mike.

And Mike is dead.

Her throat clogs as her eyes well up and she lies down next to her son, wraps her arms around him and holds tightly, trying to remember the last time he let her hold him like this, the last time they shared a hug. It feels like years. When did he stop being her little boy? How had she missed the change, and could she have stopped it if she was paying attention, if she was not mired in her own misery?

If you leave me, you'll regret it. I promise you; you'll regret it.

'I regret it,' she whispers. 'I'm so sorry.' Her tears are hot on her cheeks. 'I regret it, I regret it. I'm sorry.

'I'm sorry.' She squeezes her child, holding him close. 'I'm so sorry.'

They were supposed to be safe here.

They were supposed to be safe.

She is biting down on her lip as she cries, her arms wrapped around her son. She holds him tighter and tighter, remembering him at one and five and seven, remembering the child he was before he grew taller than her and became the angry eleven-year-old boy who hated her. She can feel that his shoulders have broadened since she last hugged him like this. She has no idea what kind of man he would have been and she will not get the chance to find out. Not all men are awful as Caroline seems to think. There are lots of wonderful men in the world. Amanda thinks of her own father, who died when she was thirty. She remembers him holding Jordan for the first time, remembers his look of awe as he gazed down at his grandson. He was a good man, a kind man, a man who loved her with everything he had. Jordan could have grown up to be the kind of man her father was. He was angry but he was still young. He didn't have to grow up to be Mike.

He cannot be gone. She cannot fathom it. How will she survive this?

And then she realises that she will probably not survive this, that she will die down here in this crazy woman's basement. It's a stunning thought. This is where she will die.

If she doesn't resist, will it happen quickly? Will Caroline just leave her here or will she come down the stairs and finish the job, and if she does, could Amanda overpower her?

Perhaps Gemma will be the one to come down and end Amanda's life.

At least Kiera is safely with Sasha. What will happen to Kiera, who is still so young? Maybe Paula will take her. More tears appear as she thinks of her sister, far away in the UK. Paula will take care of Kiera.

She tries to imagine Kiera finding out that both her parents and her brother are gone but the thought won't take hold. How will Kiera survive that? Really how?

Does it have to end this way? How long till dawn? Will the police come here to look for her? Do the police, who were supposed to be watching her, have any idea that she is not in her house? Obviously not. She should have gone to them, should have shown them the article and made them confront Caroline.

She feels her body relax, and her grip on her son loosens. She's made so many mistakes. Lifting her hand she strokes his face, feeling the softness of his skin, as a sob catches in her throat. He never even got old enough to have to shave. He never got to date. She bites down on her lip so that she will not howl and scream. If she screams, Caroline will come down here and find a way to end Amanda's life, and she needs to be with her son for as long as she can. He is gone but his body is still warm.

Still warm, she thinks. The basement is cold and he is lying on the cement floor as she is and yet... his cheek is warm. She strokes it again, her hand brushing over his eyes, feeling his soft full lashes that everyone always said were 'wasted on a boy'. Did he know what had happened to his father? Did he see Mike lying on the floor?

At least he opened the door. Mike was not a good man but Amanda knows that in his last minutes alive, he knew that he needed to let Jordan out. He was a good father in some ways. A bad husband and a bad man but he loved his children in his own way and his last thought was for his son.

And as she moves her hand across her son's face, she feels a slight flutter, a butterfly's kiss of movement.

'Jordan,' she whispers, putting her mouth close to his ear, 'Jordan,' she breathes, and in her arms, she feels the rest of his body move and a soft groan escapes his lips: 'Mum.' The word is dry and cracked with thirst. He has been here for nearly twenty-four hours now. How long has he been unconscious for? She hit him with a hammer. It's a wonder that she did not kill him. What kind of a woman could hurt a child, what kind of a mother?

'Oh, baby,' she whispers, 'I'm here. I'm here, sweetheart, I'm here.'

She waits for him to speak again but he is silent. She cannot even begin to contemplate the level of psychosis Caroline suffers from to be able to do this.

He is suffering and her whole body prickles with terror at what he has gone through. He must have been so afraid.

A surge of fury moves through her. Who is this crazy woman and how has no one stopped her yet? Amanda sits up and looks around again, seeking an escape, something that will help them get out of here. Did Caroline think she was actually helping? Did she just want to get rid of one more bad man? How does someone make themselves judge and jury like that and think they can get away with it?

Amanda stands, her ankle shrieking with pain. She must have twisted it as she fell but she needs to be upright, needs to find a way out. She cannot let the pain stop her.

'Mum,' groans Jordan again, and she thinks about mothers who lift the cars off their babies. She will be that for her son.

She and her son will not die in this mad woman's basement.

'Mum,' Jordan groans again, and she moves, despite her throbbing head, despite the fact that pain shoots up her leg.

'I'm here, baby, I'm here and I'm going to get help. I promise I'm going to get help.'

The window is high up and too small to climb out of but maybe, just maybe, she can attract attention from someone other than Gemma, other than Caroline.

The police car is just there, right there. It feels close enough to touch but it's not. It's a long shot and probably dangerous but she cannot just sit here and wait. Her son needs her.

She moves across the floor slowly to the chest of drawers, praying that it is empty and light enough to push.

When she gets there, she touches it and moves it and swallows a scream of joy that it is empty. Sending a prayer into the universe, she moves it slowly across the floor to minimise any noise. It must be nearly dawn. Through the small window she can see the shimmery pink of the false dawn that comes before the sun rises. The detectives will be here soon. *Please come very soon, please, please.* The street will be filled with people and even if she cannot attract the attention of the police car, someone will hear her, someone has to hear her.

How hard is it to break a window? What in here could break a window? Are there tools anywhere? Before she does anything else, she makes her way slowly around the basement, gingerly touching the things she can't quite see, wary of something sharp but also hoping for something sharp, but there's nothing. Caroline has obviously thought of that. She stops in front of the rack with rows and rows of pickle jars. Lifting one up, she raises and lowers it, feeling its heft and weight. If she can throw it hard enough, it could break a window, she is sure of it. Moving cautiously, she makes her way back to the chest of drawers, placing the jar on top.

She is clambering up onto the chest of drawers, one agonising step at a time, when she hears the sound of a door unlocking. She leans down and frantically lifts the jar onto the windowsill, where it wobbles slightly, and her heart races as she steadies it, hoping it stays there.

'What do you think you're doing?' Light floods into the basement from upstairs. 'Just what do you think you're doing?'

THIRTY-SEVEN

Caroline

She turns to look at me and I shine the beam from the torch I am carrying in her eyes, watching as she squints, but she doesn't stop moving, instead clambering up onto the top of the chest of drawers she has moved under the window.

I was so relieved when she hit her head. I thought it was done. But there is always mess left over and things to clean up.

'Now stop this,' I say as I walk down the stairs towards her, 'stop this right now and we can just talk.' I show her my other hand, where I am carrying the knife. She wouldn't want me to get too close to her boy with the knife in my hand.

'You need to let us go,' she says, even as she keeps moving.

'Get down or I will hurt the boy,' I tell her, waving the knife in the direction of his limp form, and I watch her face contort. She believes I will do it and I will. She obediently climbs down and moves over to the boy, putting herself protectively in front of him. 'How sweet,' I say, 'but really, Amanda, I can't see why you're protecting him. He will grow up to be just like his awful father and he will hurt someone like your husband hurt you.

Isn't it better then to stop it all before it starts? To do away with the awful boys before they become awful men? Mike is gone now and you and Kiera can move back home and live a life of peace and happiness. Isn't that what you want? It's what we all want. It's what Mary and Gemma and I have achieved. Poor Mary needs to live in a fantasy of her son still being alive but she has a kind of peace now and you can have it too. You can have a lovely life with your daughter. I can make that happen for you. I really can.' I see a momentary flash of something on her face – hope?

Yes, I decide, it's hope that she can live a serene life, and if I can just get through to her, she will go and leave this boy to me to deal with. I am sure if she were to be asked, and she was willing to tell the truth, she would admit that she loves her daughter more than her son. Mothers don't always love their children. My mother loved me in her own way but I found it very hard with Janine. I kept waiting for that feeling, for the rush of pure love that I was supposed to feel. I'm still waiting. But I took very good care of her and she doesn't appreciate it. Children are considered blessings but some of them are curses.

I can get rid of Amanda's curse if she will let me.

'Just imagine it,' I say soothingly, 'just imagine how easy your life will be with just Kiera. You will have money and time; you will have her love. You'll have everything.'

Amanda squares her shoulders as though she means to fight me and I sigh. She's going to be difficult.

'You're psychotic. And if you come near him, I will kill you, I promise I will kill you.'

'Really?' I laugh. There is blood on her face from the cut and from where she hit her head and I can see that she's hurt her ankle. 'I doubt you could kill a fly at this point.'

She hangs her head as the heavy truth settles over her. I can see that she is defeated, lost. I can see that she's given up and I'm so grateful for that. People who have lost all hope are so much easier to kill. Liam barely put up a fight at all. I experience a shiver of delightful anticipation. The first time I took a life, Liam's life, I almost couldn't do it, almost stopped myself and called the ambulance so that he would be saved.

I sat next to his bed, watching as he struggled to keep his eyes open, to hold on to his life, and I felt some pity for him, for the man he had been. But I stayed strong and did what had to be done. I fed him the pills two at a time, every few minutes. I kept telling him he hadn't had them and he was confused enough to keep taking them from me, even as he called me a 'whore' and a 'bitch'. It took everything I had to remain patient, to wait for him to take his final breath, to listen for his parting rattle. And then I heard it. I liked the sound he made as he left this world. I leaned over him, pulling one eye open, and I was fortunate enough to catch the exact moment the light went out and I knew he was gone. There is beauty in that and it is a beauty I crave more and more often. Beauty and fear.

I saw fear in Rod's eyes as he ran along the road after his wife, fear when his head swung around and he saw the headlights of the car coming towards him, fear when he knew he was going to get hit. I stopped my car and got out afterwards, grateful for the late hour and the empty road. He had gone for a run at 7 p.m. exactly as Gemma told the police. But he had returned at 8 p.m. as he usually did. Instead of showering, he hadn't changed out of his running clothes, preferring to sweat all over Gemma's furniture as he always did, just to upset her. At around 8:30 p.m., she made him a drink filled with pills to slow him down and then goaded him into an argument, knowing that he would want to hit her but also knowing that she had left the front door open, that she was ready to run and that she was faster than Rod. It all worked perfectly and I remember the exhilaration of feeling my car hit his loathsome body, the large thump that, it must be said, caused some damage to my bumper. But that's what insurance is for.

I knew there were no cameras around and I walked over to him and I caught it, just as his light blinked out, I caught it.

Now, I move slowly towards Amanda, watchful in case she leaps onto me. I give convincing her one last try. 'If you leave now, you can go to your daughter. You can go back to your lovely home in your own lovely suburb and all will be well. You know how difficult this boy will be when he's older, how he will rage at you and maybe even begin to hurt you and his sister. You know this. Let me help you find a better life, Amanda. I will make things peaceful for you and that's what you want, isn't it?'

'I don't know...' I can see she's conflicted, that she is not sure what she wants, not sure if she should just leave him. I can see the idea of a harmonious life with her daughter beckoning to her. My relationship with my daughter would certainly have been easier if Liam had died earlier. Janine would have loved me best and not her useless father. She would have loved me best, even though I was sometimes harsh with her, even though I couldn't really love her. It wasn't my fault. My mother's voice, my mother's actions would spill out of me when I was angry. It wasn't my fault.

'Come along now,' I say, 'we can sort all this out, come along now.' I speak gently, softly, and I can see that she is going to let me get close to her. I will put my hands around her neck when she does or I will use the knife but that creates mess and I hate mess. I think that when I have her, I can drop the knife and then I will squeeze the life out of her. Ironically, she will probably allow me to kill her to save the child. Some mothers feel that way about their children but it is a feeling that I was never bothered by. And once I'm done, without her, I can enjoy watching the boy die. 'Come along.' I hold out my hand, and she leans slightly forward.

'There's only one way out of here,' I whisper. 'Only one way.'

THIRTY-EIGHT

Amanda

Caroline is walking slowly towards her, her hand held out and her voice soft and comforting. Amanda's head pounds and her ankle throbs. She cannot get this wrong. Caroline needs to put down the knife. Amanda cannot fight a knife.

How long can she keep this woman talking? How long can she stay calm and let this lunatic think that she's getting to her, that the idea of a life with just her and Kiera is what she wants?

'He's my... son,' she says softly.

'Yes, but he's going to hurt you. You already know he's going to hurt you.'

Amanda cocks her head. 'But maybe... maybe he'll grow up to be a good man.'

Caroline chuckles as she slowly moves closer. Amanda knows that she is not going to be allowed to leave here alive, knows that Caroline is just trying to get close enough to hurt her, to kill her. Caroline needs to be close and Amanda needs time, and as the sun rises up higher in the sky and more light begins to flood the basement, Amanda resolves to be the one who wins.

'There are no good men.' Caroline's voice is low and harsh, her hand waving the knife. 'I've never known one in my life. Mary's son was already an abuser just like his father. If he had been allowed to live, he would have hurt his mother until he found a woman stupid enough to marry him so he could hurt her. He was already filled with anger and hate. There are no good men, Amanda,' she repeats and Amanda tries a small nod, a small sign of acquiescence even as she listens for another car arriving.

Is the police car still there? Are the detectives on their way? If she makes a move and there is no one to help her, she will not survive. That's the truth.

'Caroline, listen.'

'Enough talking now,' snaps Caroline. 'I'm very tired. Take my hand and we will leave and you can go to your daughter.' She holds out her hand and Amanda lifts hers, not to take it but to buy some more time.

'Put down the knife, please, you're scaring me. If you put the knife down, we can talk some more about bad men because you're right. Mike was bad and Jordan is just so angry all the time and I do worry about him hurting Kiera. I do worry about that.' Amanda hangs her head, showing Caroline that she is weak, defeated.

'All right.' Caroline places the weapon on a shelf next to her.

Amanda leans forward a little more, as though she means to take Caroline's hand, and then she hears it, the sound of a door slamming, a car door slamming. It carries through the basement window and she is close enough to hear it. *Did I hear that or did I just want to hear it?*

'We can have a cup of tea. I bet you'd like a cup of tea.' *Did Caroline hear that?*

Amanda nods her head. She would like a cup of tea. She would like to sit in a chair and sip tea, and she remembers the cup of tea she shared with Caroline, when she let her defences down and confessed her struggles. Shame washes over her at her own stupidity and at the thought she had that perhaps Caroline would be someone to talk to as she navigated her divorce.

But this is not someone to talk to, to confide in, to trust. This is not even a person walking towards her, and if she takes her hand, she will die. And Jordan will die. Her own death is of no consequence but she cannot let this psychopath steal her son's life. Caroline's eyes dart to the side. She did hear the car door. The woman has stepped away from the shelf with the knife but her body turns slightly to retrieve it.

It's real. They're here. And I have one chance to survive this.

A man's laugh fills the air. Is it Detective Chen or someone else? It doesn't matter. If Amanda screams, they will hear her. But the knife is only a step away from Caroline's hand.

How can help be so close and so impossibly far away?

'Come on. We don't want any more men here, do we? We don't need another man telling us what to do. Come on.'

'No,' says Amanda.

'No?' the woman asks, surprised.

'Let me go, let my son go.' She can hear that her voice is weak, that she is weak. She is scared.

'Well, then.' Caroline drops her hand and shines the torch over at Jordan, who is ragdoll loose, his limbs splayed. 'I'll just start with him.' She moves back towards the shelf to pick up the knife.

Did you know, Mum? Did you know, right, that sometimes a mum can be so strong, like so strong that she can lift a whole giant car off her baby, did you know that, Mum? Five-year-old Jordan's voice is in her head, his faith in her abilities, in the abilities of every mum to take care of a child, absolute and clear and filled with trust.

She opens her mouth and screams, 'Help me, help us, help, help,' and as she does, she turns and leaps onto the chest of drawers, almost falling but pulling herself up, the pain from her ankle ripping through her whole body. She pounds on the window, her hand in a fist. 'Detective, detective, detective,' she screams, pounding hard. 'Someone help, anyone help!' She pounds on the window.

'Get down, you witch,' she hears and Caroline grabs at her pants. 'I will kill this boy, now get down.'

Amanda kicks her off and then she pounds on the window again, and then the pickle jar on the windowsill begins to wobble and she grabs it before it falls. As Caroline pulls at her pants she moves her arm back, the jar heavy, slippery in her sweaty hand. She has one chance, just one, and in that moment, she thinks, *Help me, Mike, help me save our son.*

With every bit of strength she has left, she throws the jar, knowing that it may not go through the window.

But the jar connects with the glass and punches through, glass shattering and falling over Amanda, tiny shards slicing into her skin.

Caroline pulls her down but Amanda gives it one last try and kicks out at her, obviously connecting with something as Caroline shouts, 'Ow, bitch.' And Amanda can see that the knife is in her hand again. *I'm going to die. I'm going to die but it's okay because Jordan will live.*

Amanda stands again, pulling herself onto the chest of drawers in seconds, and then she uses her hand to punch at the pieces of glass left on the window, cutting the skin, feeling the knife blade sink into the back of her leg as she does. Her body sags but adrenalin keeps her standing.

'Detective, help, help, help!' she screams, long and loud, her voice growing hoarse.

'Nasty bitch,' screeches Caroline behind her, and her hands claw at Amanda's legs again but Amanda kicks out and she screams again. *A mother can lift a car to save her child. She can lift a car and smash a window.*

And then her body is pulled down and she feels herself fall, her head hitting the cement floor, the crack exploding through her skull.

THIRTY-NINE

Jordan

I keep my eyes closed because it's too hard to open them but I can hear her screaming, hear her begging for help.

I feel her fall, feel the air change, and then her body is next to mine and her arm flops over my chest and she lies very still.

I love you, Mum, I want to say but can't.

Don't leave me, Mum! I want to shout but my voice is trapped in the fog swirling through my brain.

'Oh, dearie me,' the old woman says and then she laughs.

I did this. I know I did. I shouldn't have left, shouldn't have run away to my dad. And he didn't even care. I know that. He picked me up because he knew it would hurt her. 'She'll suffer for this,' he kept saying as he drove me home and I was scared then. Too scared to do anything except what he told me to do. She ran away from him to save herself, to save us, and then I did this.

And now it will be over. I let the fog fill every space inside me. Her arm is heavy on my body. Is she gone? I think she's gone and I'm next. The fog is nearly everywhere now and I wait for it to be over.

'Stupid, wicked boy,' I hear the old lady sneer.

But now a man is shouting, 'Stop, stop right there, put the knife down. Don't move. Drop the knife, don't move, drop the knife now.'

'Oh, Detective... Detective, I found—'

'Stop talking, back away, back away now.'

A clang sound fills my ears. Was that a knife? She was going to stab me with a knife. Did she stab my mum? Is my mum dead? I killed her. I did this and I killed my mum. I let the grey fog fill up every cell in my body. I don't want to be alive if my mum is dead.

I let myself sink. There is no pain and the fog is nice. I stay in the fog.

I am jolted awake, light is everywhere, noise, sirens, shouting and I am moving.

'It's okay, it's okay,' someone says right into my ear.

I try to open my eyes and then there is pain on my skin.

'It's okay,' says the voice, 'just giving you some fluids. It's okay, you're fine.'

'Mum,' I whisper, the word coming from deep inside me.

Mums can lift cars off their kids if they have to. I know that. But can they stop crazy people? I don't think so.

Something cool runs across my face.

'That's better,' says the voice.

'Mum?' I ask her, my eyes struggling to open.

'Your mum is in the ambulance behind us and you're going to be fine. She saved you.'

'She... saved... me,' I say. She saved me.

She lifted the car. She stopped the crazy person. She saved me.

EPILOGUE

Amanda

She's not sure when she will get used to it, used to the lack of fear. The funeral was ten days ago and the visitors have petered off and the children have returned to school and suddenly, she is alone here in this large house. It used to be her house and it was a home that she loved because she chose everything inside it, but now that she is here, surrounded by her things, it feels like it belongs to someone else. She is a different person now.

She cannot get used to the fact that Mike is not here, that he will never be here again. Sometimes, the wind will slam an open door closed and she will jump and her heart will race and she will feel the constriction of panic in her chest because she's certain that he's back, that he's home and that she will surely pay for leaving him in the first place.

But Mike is gone. And everything belongs to her. Patricia is running the shop now, telling her to take as much time as she needs. She doesn't know how much time she will need. She's not sure if she wants to take over the shop or sell it. She's not sure if she wants to live in this house or sell it, live in this suburb or move. She's not sure of anything at all. She wasn't sure the children should return to school but Paula suggested she leave it up to them and they wanted to go. It's a new school year for both of them and they were not equipped to just be at home. It's better that they are surrounded by their friends and she can only hope that because the funeral was ten days ago, their classmates will have already moved on. They are the TikTok generation after all. Jordan and Kiera will never move on, not completely.

There are moments of horrible guilt and shame. Guilt that she took her children to a place that nearly resulted in Jordan's death. And shame that she put herself first, that her safety was more important than theirs.

'You had no idea,' Paula said to her over and again when she came for the funeral. 'How could you have?' And logically Amanda knows that's true but logic doesn't always come into it.

She chose the street for a reason, a reason that she never wants to have to reveal, ever, to anyone.

The message she thought would end her marriage has been deleted from her phone now but she will never forget the words.

> *You don't know me but I know who you are and I need to tell you. Mike and I are in love. He told me you won't give him a divorce but I'm begging you, just let him go.*

She was ready to let him go but *he* wasn't ready to let *her* go and she felt she had no choice but to run, to hide, but to hide somewhere that would give her some leverage when he arrived. West Street was that place. It never occurred to her that West Street could be the dangerous place it turned out to be.

She is sitting in the garden today with a cup of tea and a piece of cake. The freezer is filled with cakes and casseroles and it feels like she will never have to cook again.

The cake is chocolate, rich and very sweet, but she is eating it anyway. Soon it will be time to get the children from school and then the afternoon will be taken up with homework – and Jordan also has therapy today.

The therapist has an office opposite a park so she and Kiera will spend the hour there. She will run and jump and climb and Amanda will watch her, filled with guilt and shame over everything that happened. And when she goes to get her son, walking across the road will be painful on her still healing ankle and she will feel the pulling of her scar tissue on her leg and be reminded, in that moment, of everything that happened, as she is reminded constantly, no matter what she's doing.

Her own therapist wants her to work on letting go of guilt and fear and shame, of everything. She has a long way to go. All she really needs to know is that the children are safe right now.

Mike picked Jordan up on West Street, away from the cul-de-sac, at 8 p.m. Jordan had been in their family home the whole time, and when the bell rang at midnight, Mike told Jordan it was his mother and told him to hide in the safe room until she was gone. Mike thought she had noticed her child was not in bed and had come to claim him. It was what Mike had wanted, and even now, Amanda will never know what would have happened to her if she had rung the bell, had walked into the house looking for Jordan, if she had gone and demanded the passports. Perhaps she would be dead today.

Jordan does not remember much about the basement. He remembers the door to the safe room opening and Gemma standing there, a look of shock and terror on her face and a hammer in her hand. He remembers her coming towards him, even as she wailed, 'I'm sorry.'

'I woke up and I was cold and I was thirsty and I wanted to get up but my body wouldn't move, and then I was nowhere again.'

He remembers the ambulance ride to the hospital and the paramedic who was kind and made him feel safe.

He is very different to the boy who moved to West Street only five weeks ago.

He is subdued, sad and alarmingly compliant. She hopes that doesn't last forever even though she doesn't want the aggressive child he was to return.

Both children miss their father and she is trying to give them space to talk about him, to revisit happy memories. Do they need to know the truth of what went on behind their closed bedroom door? Perhaps but perhaps not. They are still too young and she cannot share it with them. She has a feeling that Jordan may know more than Kiera. In a conversation last week about buying him a gaming computer, he said, 'Dad wanted me to have one even though you didn't want me to,' and she replied, 'I know that.'

'He would have made you buy me one,' said Jordan softly, and she heard not a threat but a simple sadness in his tone. He definitely knows more than she wants to contemplate. Both he and Kiera now have phones, for better or worse. She needs to know that they can always get hold of her.

She is only thirty-five and she can acknowledge that when she looks in the mirror but she feels like her whole life is over. That's also something she is working on with her therapist.

There will be a trial or trials at some point. Caroline will have to pay for her crime. Amanda will have to testify as will Jordan, but the public prosecutor has assured them that he will not have to be in the courtroom with Caroline.

Gemma is a more complicated situation.

If she goes to prison, her girls will have to go and live in the US with grandparents they have only met a handful of times or they will have to go into the foster system. They have an aunt here, Rod's much older sister, and they are with her now but she doesn't want them full time, can't have them full time. If they live in the US, they will not be able to see their mother.

Caroline was driving the car that killed Rod but she made

Gemma believe that the whole thing had been her plan. Amanda watched Gemma's first court appearance via a video link and was shocked at how frail she looks now with her brown roots showing through her blonde hair. She doesn't want to feel sympathy for the woman who killed Mike and who nearly killed Jordan. Gemma should go to prison for a long time. But she feels terribly sorry for her girls, who returned home from camp to find their world upended. There are no real happy endings here, just endings.

Gemma hurt others. At some point it can't be forgiven and it has to stop.

Hopefully, by the time he has to testify, Jordan will be stronger and Amanda will be too.

Checking the time, she picks up the plate with the half-eaten piece of cake and her empty cup of tea and returns to the kitchen.

Before she gets her keys to go and pick up her children, she stops in front of the fridge and gazes at the family photograph there, taken on their last holiday, only six months ago.

Mike and the children are smiling widely as they stand with their backs to the ocean. Mike has one arm wrapped around the children and one arm wrapped around her. She is smiling too. But she has her hand resting on her stomach, because there was a large dark bruise forming there from the night before when he punched her. She can see how fake her smile is, how much pain she was actually in.

Her hands move without her thinking and she takes the picture and tears it in two and throws it out.

She will print out another picture for the fridge, one with just the three of them, one when she is really smiling, really happy, really her.

But now she will get her children from school and listen to their tales about their days and they will go on together. Just the way they should.

And she will not allow the words she said to Caroline as she detailed Mike's abuse to circle in her head. *I really wish something would happen to him. I really wish he was dead.* She will dismiss them from her mind and go on with her life.

Caroline

I miss my garden the most. I miss sitting on the deck on a warm summer's day with a glass of wine.

And I miss Luna, oh how I miss Luna.

Gemma's daughters are living with their aunt and taking care of Luna now. It's strange to think that by the time I get out of prison, she will be gone, although I have no idea how long I will be sentenced for.

I do not see Gemma. They have sent us to different prisons and I am sure she will pin as much of what happened as she can on me. Let her try. I have my own story to tell, and when necessary, I can look like the frail elderly lady I would like a jury to see me as. I do not look forward to hearing Amanda testify. Her son will not have much to say. He was more or less unconscious the whole time.

What frustrates me is that I was going to do the right thing. I wasn't the one who hurt him and I was waiting for a quiet time so that I could move him to nearby bush. I was even going to find him for everyone. I was going to be a hero. And now I will be going to prison.

All I wanted was to live in a nice quiet street, to be surrounded by lovely neighbours and have some peace, especially after all those terrible months with Liam when he became so abusive and then his death.

I remember the first time he hit me, my terrible shock at that was overwhelming. I know he was sick and perhaps he didn't mean it but I also knew that some part of him understood what he was doing. He was getting back at me, thinking that his illness gave him impunity. I suffered in silence for months, only mentioning it to the nurse who came to help. But what could I do? You cannot abandon a sick man because women are supposed to be the carers, the nurturers of the world regardless of what those we care for throw at us. And so I was trapped. Janine would never have forgiven me. And now she will never speak to me again. She sent me a letter. Just one single sentence on a piece of paper:

You got what you deserve.

I moved after Liam died and met Gemma and I saw that everywhere in the world are terrible men hurting women, taking out their anger and frustration on those who are weaker than them. And that made me furious.

My mother suffering through my father's abuse was always with me and then when Liam became abusive, I felt her pain inside me.

And Gemma's pain was written all over her face, all over her body, and I knew that Rod would move on to his daughters one day; indeed, he had already started looking for reasons to hit them. They look just like their mother used to.

I thought that once Rod was gone, that would be the end of it, that peace would reign in our quiet street and all would be well.

But then Cora went to the nursing home and her house was sold and there was Amanda and her tale of woe.

I feel terribly sorry for Mary. We have always understood each other. But then we have known each other for a long time. Helping me care for Liam was her job. She was always kind and patient but I could see that her spirit was broken, her life destroyed. She used to stay longer than the assigned time some days and we would talk and drink tea and tell each other our stories in the way that women always have.

I was lucky that she was the person the agency assigned, lucky that she knew how hard it was to be a woman married to a terrible man. I didn't even have to explain it to her. She saw the bruises when she came to bathe my sick husband and she heard the way he spoke to me, understood the terrible undercurrent of vicious anger in his nasty words.

She knew Liam was going to die anyway and I just sent him along ahead of schedule. She told the police that he had expressed his wish to die many times. A white lie that we kept between us.

And then when everything was over, she told me about a small house in her street that was for sale and it felt perfect. A new start next to a close friend. She will be lonely now.

Gemma didn't want to do anything to Mike but she owed me. She will always owe me.

I still feel I have done the right thing. Terrible men cannot be allowed to get away with their misdeeds. They need to be punished and I am grateful that I have been able to mete out that punishment.

All I am doing is trying to make the world a better place in my own way.

I like to think that whatever the courts and society say, I have succeeded in doing that. That's what I like to think.

I'm quite famous now. The press are using words like 'sociopath' and 'psychopath'. The last time they wrote about me, after Liam's death, I was quite upset about it. I didn't like the idea that people were judging me.

But it feels different this time. Especially because of the letters from other women. Women who have been abused and hurt, women who have secretly plotted revenge in the quiet hours of the night as they nursed their bruises. We can be pushed too far. Men don't expect that. They think that when they beat us, they defeat us, but they don't.

Certainly, Amanda was struggling and scared. But I know

that when she confessed her troubles to me, when she told me what her husband did to her and how she had run from him, she understood that I would help her.

I really wish something would happen to him. I really wish he was dead. She said those words to me as she stood up to leave my kitchen after confessing exactly what she was dealing with.

'I think Gemma felt the same way,' I told her. 'And she got... lucky.'

'Yes,' she agreed, 'very lucky. If only I could get that lucky,' and then she looked at me for a long time and I knew that she knew what she was asking.

And I gave it to her.

Now I will pay the price for that because she will deny saying it. It takes a very strong person to admit what they want, what they really, truly want, and to make sure it happens.

I was there for the women who couldn't make it happen, and sometimes when the shouts of other women wake me in here, instead of getting upset, I congratulate myself on what I have achieved.

I was strong enough. I made it happen.

It helps me get back to sleep. It gives me peace and that's all I've ever really wanted. Peace.

Gemma

When the police knocked at my door, I was ready.

I knew to ask for a lawyer. And when I do tell my story, I will paint the perfect picture of an abused woman who turned to a neighbour for help. A psychopathic neighbour who then threatened her and forced her to go and confront a violent man.

I could have said no, could have simply refused to do what Caroline wanted me to do.

I am not capable of murder. I was not capable of murder.

Not until I realised who Amanda was.

Even now, the queasiness that appeared in my stomach the day I looked up Amanda Caldwell while Mary and Caroline watched on has not truly left me.

It's a common enough surname. That's what I hoped as I searched Instagram and Facebook, that it was all just a coincidence and had nothing to do with me.

But there he was, Michael Caldwell, my Michael Caldwell.

The 'terrible wife' Mike always talked about had somehow moved into my street and soon she was telling a very different story to the one I knew.

He never hurt me. He only loved me, showering me with gifts that I kept hidden and promises of the future we would have together. I believed he deserved better than his wife, that he deserved someone who would love him the way he should be loved. He deserved me.

I met him at work. He was looking for men's clothing and couldn't find the right section. Or he just said that, lied about that. I thought he was single until I understood that he wasn't, but by then I didn't care. I thought I'd hit the jackpot. When we were together, he would tell me how cold his wife was, how indifferent, how much she disliked her own children.

I didn't message him to tell him I'd met her. Perhaps if he had been in the country, I would have gone to him, would have revealed where she was. But he was away. And I didn't tell her who I was but I wonder now if she knew, if she was in my street for a reason. I think she knew.

I kept away from her, from Amanda, just watching, just listening to Caroline's and Mary's tales about the family, collecting the information to share with Mike at the best time. I didn't want to know her better. I needed her to stay 'the wife', callous and cruel.

The way her son behaved seemed to be a sign of something, of bad mothering.

I knew that one day, I was going to be a better wife to Mike and I would even be a better mother to his children.

Caroline thought she was sending me there to do her bidding but I went for myself.

I went there that night to tell him that I knew Amanda wanted to leave, that I had met the cold, indifferent wife and that all he had to do was grant her the divorce and then we would be together as we had been planning. Caroline wanted Amanda gone and she thought killing Mike was the solution, but I knew that all I had to do was convince Mike to be gracious about the divorce and then we would all move on with our lives. I would live in the big beautiful house and wear the designer clothes. I would replace Amanda and I would be better at being Mike's wife so he would never be angry. He would never hurt me.

Sometimes a lesson needs to be learned more than once.

I know that now because that's when it all unravelled.

He was not overjoyed to see me. He was furious.

'We can be together now,' I told him. 'She doesn't want to be with you anymore and it will be easy. I've even met your kids and they'll love my kids and we can be a family.' I was stupidly painting pictures in my head and I had no idea who he was. Just like his first wife, just like his second wife.

But Mike had no desire for a third wife.

'As if I would trade her in for you,' he laughed. 'She's a whole different class of woman compared to you.' His eyes roamed up and down my body, the body that he had, only weeks before, called 'magnificent'.

And for a second, I was back in my bedroom with Rod years ago. I was standing in a bathing suit, waiting for his opinion as he laughed and sneered at how skinny I was, at how the suit bagged around my flat chest, at how unattractive I looked.

And that's when I became someone who could kill a man.

I was a small, timid mouse once and I remade myself into a

glamorous Barbie doll but I still wasn't enough for a man to love, really love. To love and not to hurt.

I was glad to have the hammer, glad to be able to shout and scream and swing it with force.

I didn't think the boy would be there.

I didn't think Caroline would take things so far.

And now I am here and my roots are already showing and the clothes they have given me sag around my body because I cannot stomach the food.

I am turning back into the mouse, timid and small, easy to hurt.

I am the mouse again because she came to our street with her unruly children and her baggage.

She was the wrong kind of person for our cul-de-sac, the kind of woman who should have stayed away and left us all alone.

But we only knew that at the end.

We only know it now.

A LETTER FROM NICOLE

Hello,

I would like to thank you for taking the time to read *Welcome to West Street*. If you enjoyed this novel and want to keep up to date with all my latest releases, just sign up at the following link. Your email address will never be shared and you can unsubscribe at any time.

www.bookouture.com/nicole-trope

This novel shifted and changed as I was writing it and I have to say that, at some point, I was as surprised by the ending as I think some readers may be.

I want to echo Amanda's thoughts that there are many good men in the world. I have a father, a brother, a husband and a son and I know them to be wonderful men.

I loved creating the character of Caroline. I didn't realise quite how deep her psychosis went until well into the novel, and while I know many people won't be able to relate to her terrible anger at men, some will. She is a character damaged by a harsh childhood from which she never recovered. And she is someone who chose to use violence as a way to deal with her own trauma.

I feel like Gemma got sucked into things but once there, she made her own decisions.

This novel doesn't have a perfect happy ending because

Amanda's children have lost a father and Gemma's daughters will lose their mother to prison, but not all endings can be perfect, as Amanda acknowledges.

I do see Amanda finding her way forward with her children – perhaps in a different house where there are no terrible memories. I felt for each of these women and what they had to deal with and I hope you will too.

As always, I will be so grateful if you leave a review for the novel, especially if you loved the book and can avoid those pesky spoilers.

I love hearing from my readers – you can get in touch on social media. I try to reply to each message I receive.

Thanks again for reading,

Nicole x

facebook.com/NicoleTrope
x.com/nicoletrope
instagram.com/nicoletropeauthor

ACKNOWLEDGEMENTS

My first thank you goes to Ellen Gleeson, whose guidance is so appreciated. I remain dedicated to finding the best prologue with you and hope we get to do so for many more books.

I would also like to thank Jess Readett for all her help with publicity. It's lovely to know I can count on you for any questions I have.

Thanks to DeAndra Lupu for the brilliant copy edit, Liz Hatherell for the very detailed proofread and Mandy Kullar for the final touches.

Thanks to the whole team at Bookouture, including Jenny Geras, Peta Nightingale, Richard King, Alba Proko, Ruth Tross and everyone else involved in producing my audio books and selling rights, and spreading the word on my novels.

Thanks to my mother, Hilary, may you be my first reader for many more years.

Thanks also to David, Mikhayla, Isabella, Jacob and Jax.

And once again thank you to those who read, review and blog about my work and contact me on social media to let me know you loved the book. I love hearing your stories and reasons why you have connected with a novel.

Every review is appreciated and I do read them all.

PUBLISHING TEAM

Turning a manuscript into a book requires the efforts of many people. The publishing team at Bookouture would like to acknowledge everyone who contributed to this publication.

Audio
Alba Proko
Sinead O'Connor
Melissa Tran

Commercial
Lauren Morrissette
Hannah Richmond
Imogen Allport

Cover design
Lisa Horton

Data and analysis
Mark Alder
Mohamed Bussuri

Editorial
Ellen Gleeson
Nadia Michael

Copyeditor
DeAndra Lupu

Proofreader
Liz Hatherell

Marketing
Alex Crow
Melanie Price
Occy Carr
Cíara Rosney
Martyna Młynarska

Operations and distribution
Marina Valles
Stephanie Straub
Joe Morris

Production
Hannah Snetsinger
Mandy Kullar
Ria Clare
Nadia Michael

Publicity
Kim Nash
Noelle Holten
Jess Readett
Sarah Hardy

Rights and contracts
Peta Nightingale
Richard King
Saidah Graham